LORD HORNINGTON'S ACADEMY OF LOVE

Young Eve shivered and sighed. I could see the pulse racing in her neck as I seated her on the chaise longue and knelt down behind her. 'You have the most beautiful breasts,' I murmured. 'May I remove the bodice of your dress?'

I lifted the bust bodice and rested it gently on the tops of those adorable breasts; the swelling of her nipples looked almost painful to me as I rubbed them in big, gentle circles against my palms. Then, increasing the pressure, I turned her and eased her down until she was half lying on the seat.

The sight of a young girl, a virgin, lying back half-clothed in such a lascivious position, is vastly stimulating – better than a stupendous win at cards even. I became more determined than ever to make her realize how fortunate she was to have chosen me as her tutor in these arts . . .

Also available from Headline:

Eros in the Country
Eros in the Town
Eros on the Grand Tour
Eros in the New World
Venus in Paris
A Lady of Quality
Sweet Fanny
Sweet Fanny's Diary
The Love Pagoda
The Education of a Maiden
Maid's Night In
Lena's Story
Cremorne Gardens
The Lusts of the Borgias

Lord Hornington's Academy of Love

Faye Rossignol

HEADLINE

First published in 1990
by HEADLINE BOOK PUBLISHING PLC

10 9 8 7 6 5 4 3 2 1

ISBN 0 7472 3432 9

Typeset in 10/12 pt English Times
by Colset Private Limited, Singapore

Printed and bound in Great Britain by
Collins, Glasgow

HEADLINE BOOK PUBLISHING PLC
Headline House
79 Great Titchfield Street
London W1P 7FN

Lord Hornington's Academy of Love

[Editor's note: To our modern taste, Victorian and Edwardian writers are long-winded, coy, and least funny when they try hardest to amuse. In editing this classic of erotic literature (I cannot call it fiction), I have sought to remove the worst of such blemishes without polishing them entirely away; enough, I hope, remains to charm the reader and preserve the essential period feeling. I have modernized the punctuation and some of the spelling but have preserved a few words whose original form is somehow right for the context.

I say I cannot call it fiction, for, as I show in my postscript, the tale you are about to read is essentially factual. But "Roger Hornington" had a lively imagination and a Münchausen-like capacity for embroidering his exploits. His male readers will, I know, derive enormous pleasure from the following pages; his female ones will, I hope – like me – find a subtler amusement in separating fact from fantasy. I recommend it as an antidote to the displeasure we feel at his revelations of so many of our amorous secrets; for, full-blooded male that he undoubtedly was, he knew rather too much about us for our comfort! – Faye R.]

If Queen Victoria hadn't died when she did, none of it would have happened. A few of us were standing idly at the club windows, looking out at that sea of black which was London in the days immediately after the demise of the dear old girl, God rest her, I suppose . . . and we were saying that, though one couldn't help feeling the odd twinge of sorrow for her family and all that rot, one was bound to heave the compensatory sigh of relief for the rest of her realm.

Everything her name had stood for could now be buried with her at Frogmore, and a new era could begin under jolly King Edward. (And, as Mrs Keppel has so often said to me, "There's no jollier man on earth to be under than *him.")* We "Edvaardians," as we will no doubt soon be known, could have our day in the sun. At the very least we could begin by taking the frilly little skirts off the piano legs; they always induced the most incandescently sexual thoughts in *me,* I must confess.

I was giving out such opinions when Tommy Champion, the world's pessimist, moaned that nothing would ever change the English . . . bulldog breed . . . teeth in – never let go. The streets would still be full of whores every night and the churches would still be packed with their customers every Sunday. *Plus ça change* . . . as my chef always says when he serves me from yesterday's menu.

I don't know how we got from there to my assertion that "thousands" of respectable middle-class parents would now sell their daughters to me. I mean, why *now?* It was true enough even in Victoria's heyday. Indeed, from their very beginnings the middles classes have always measured their girls' virginities in *£sd*. But there we are. I did open my mouth and I did make the assertion, no doubt of it. When a man has enjoyed a sexual upbringing like mine, and is, moreover blessed with an almost limitless capacity to indulge it, well, these things do rather tend to trip off the unguarded tongue. Quick as a flash Tommy had it all duly entered in the club betting book – and with a thousand guineas to back it, too. He could afford it, of course, but, even so, I hate taking money off fools.

I immediately inserted the following advertisement in the *Morning Post*:

> TITLED NOBLEWOMAN (daughter of a Marquess) requires young lady companion under 20 of impeccable character to accompany her on extensive de luxe tours of Empire, Continent, America, etc. All found and generous allowance. Large gratuity on completion of tour. Character references of the highest order will be strictly required. Replies in the applicant's own hand, with covering letter from parents or guardians, and recent portrait(s), to Box . . .

The reason for stipulating that the girl be under twenty, is obvious, I hope, for even an archbishop would gladly sell off his unmarriageable rubbish.

I received four thousand three hundred and twenty-seven replies. The Albany had an extra porter assigned until the storm was past. Tommy began to look very pale. I then put another announcement in the *Morning Post*:

> TITLED NOBLEWOMAN who advertised for lady companion for extensive tours abroad begs to advise applicants that, over four thousand replies having been received to date, no further applications can possibly be entertained. She craves the indulgence of all correspondents, whose letters will be dealt with in order of receipt.

Four thousand-plus! What had the Middle Classes been *doing?* Last time I observed them they appeared to have given up the Biggest Family Competition which had been an annual fixture in their calendar through most of the recently expired century; latterly the papers seemed to be full of complaints that army officers and clergymen would soon have to be recruited among the sons of people in trade. So how could they possibly muster four thousand nubile girls for me in less than a week? They must have had one of their wretched factories at it somewhere. Sweated labour, right enough.

I hired a typewriting agency to send out the following letter to all applicants, good, bad, or indifferent:

> Dear Mr and Mrs Chaunt *[e.g.]*,
> I regret to inform you that my sister, Lady Wilhelmina, is indisposed and will no longer be able to undertake the strenuous, though de luxe, voyages she had planned. However, by the greatest good fortune, I, her brother, will shortly be embarking on a tour of Paris, Rome, Vienna, and Constantinople and am, as it happens, seeking a lively young companion of precisely the type your daughter Susan *[say]* seems to represent – at least, as far as one can tell from her beautiful photograph. So, to avoid disappointing every single applicant, Lady Wilhelmina has kindly allowed me to take over the burden of replying to the more than four-thousand letters she has received.
>
> I may add that, generous though *her* intended remuneration was to have been, mine will be a great deal more so. To the parents of the successful applicant (who can hardly be expected, in these changed circumstances, to bear ungrudgingly the loss of their daughter's services), I am offering a thousand pounds. [*Something like £50,000 in modern currency! – FR*] and to the girl herself, £100 a week [*Say, £5,000 today – FR*] all found – plus occasional presents

of jewellery, furs, gowns, etc. The usual thing, you know. On the conclusion of the tour, some time in the summer, there will be a *bonne bouche* of a further £1,000 for her.

I must stress that a great deal will be demanded of Susan as my Companion; she will be expected to accompany me to levées, galleries, afternoon and evening performances at the opera and theatre, picnics, dinners, soirées, galas, balls, concerts, and suppers. We shall be staying only at the most select hotels, so the whole tour will be managed with the utmost prudence. My discretion begins the moment I open your reply to this proposal. And I do promise you that the strictest care will be taken to ensure that Susan does not mix in dubious company; indeed, it must be understood that she will *hardly ever* be out of my sight.

If this alternative proposal is not to your liking, please forgive my importunity and accept my apologies for the trouble to which you have been put. The young lady's photograph has been retained, awaiting your response. If nothing further has been heard from you within one month, it will be automatically returned, together with your application and reference.

Yours etc.

Roger Hornington

PS Though I bear the title Earl of Rutland, I insist upon it only with inferiors; it is quite in order for *you,* dear Mr and Mrs Chaunt, to address me as plain "Lord Roger."

I directed replies to the Etonian Club – an establishment I hardly ever visit.

And then I had nothing to do but sit back and wait.

Over the following three weeks five irate mastodons from the shires turned up brandishing horsewhips at the OE Club. Horsewhips - in 1901! The old queen was a long time cooling in her grave. Anyway, that was another guinea Tommy owed me - he bet there'd be over fifty of 'em. Also one man came bearing a bouquet of cabbages - a relation, perhaps, of the Marquess of Queensberry? I wished I'd been there to receive him, except that I could only half remember what poor dear Oscar had said to the old buffoon.

But best of all, I had *forty* replies that more or less accepted my offer! By my reckoning that means something like one per cent of respectable Middle Class parents are perfectly willing to sell their daughters into concubinage - provided the offer is high enough and the situation can be made to seem outwardly respectable.

Nor was that the end of it. At least four hundred more suggested that if I would consider taking along an elderly widow or invalid, and then enroll their daughter as that person's companion or nurse - just for the look of the thing - they would consent to the arrangement. Thirty wives replied privately, saying, in effect, "Hang my daughter, take me! I'll give you a far jollier time than she ever could." Experienced dames they were, too - all with pet names for future correspondence in the personal columns! And well over a hundred servant girls said they "couldn't help reading" my letter and they'd gladly do it for a tenth of what I was offering their master and mistress.

And there was one forlorn cry from a footman in Warrington, telling me that all women are a snare and a delusion in the end, and did I ever think of taking up with a handsome, lusty, virile, and understanding male companion? Him at least I did reply to in person:

"Often, dear boy. Next time you're in London, look me up at the Albany." Not that I'm much given to my own sex, but it makes a pleasant change, three or four times a year. And it keeps one's youthful memories alive: *Floreat Etona!*

The agency then set about replying to everyone, returning their material and regretting that little Susan, or whoever she was, did not survive the short-listing – and implying that I could not risk even the slightest spot on the reputation of a young girl who was so obviously and eminently marriageable. And that was the end of that – the easiest thousand guineas I ever earned.

Two weeks later I was just getting ready for my usual evening round of pleasure – dine at Willis's, an hour or two at the Gaiety or the Alhambra, pick up an agreeable vestal, and take her to a cigar divan or a *chambre privée* at the Café Royal – and so to a celibate and virtuous bed. I absolutely adore women and make myself an abject slave to 'em for a couple of hours practically every single night.

Anyway, I was just leaving the Albany when I became aware of an altercation going on behind me in the porter's lodge; I was anticipating my evening's sport so keenly that I probably would not have pricked up my ears if the young lady had not mentioned my name: Horn-ing-ton – and beautifully spoken, too. Though only those three mellifluous syllables rang in my memory's ear, I could tell at once that she was no importunate tart but a lady of middle-if not upper-middle-class breeding. This faculty for distinguishing between classes on hearing the utterance of but a single word is something of which we English ought to be downright ashamed – except that when one is so very good at something, it's hard to be simultaneously shamefaced about it. I feel precisely the same ambivalence toward my own sexual prowess, indeed.

I glanced back. She half turned to face me. The porter vigorously shook his head at me behind her. But not far enough behind her, for she saw him; her face at once broke into a radiant smile. "My dear Lord Hornington!" She advanced toward me, hand outstretched.

I am not easily swayed by a pretty face. The plainest girls have their claims on my heart, too. Their breasts are as soft, their flesh as silken, their vertical smile as warm – and often more inviting; their hearts, too – their *need* for loving tenderness is as great as if not greater than that of their prettier sisters. Their gratitude is certainly much larger.

So I remained cool as she approached; I was able to observe that she was one of the most ravishing young fillies I ever clapped eyes on, and yet I was no more moved by it than by any other encounter of a similarly promiscuous nature.

"I'm afraid I do not seem . . ." I began diffidently.

She put me out of my dilemma. "Indeed we have never met, sir, but until very recently you kept my photograph always by you. And when you returned it to my parents you were kind enough to say the most complimentary things about me."

"Aha, yes, in that case . . ."

"Allow me to introduce myself – I am Eve Bassington. My father is James Bassington of Bassington and Bassington (he's the second one) in the Wirral – too far away, I fear, for him to effect this introduction in person."

I raised her hand to within an inch of my lips and murmured charmed or something. But now I could not take my eyes off her. A beautiful woman viewed across a crowded room, or even an uncrowded entrance hall, is, as it were, a picture, a chimaera, a remote and uncertain commodity. But when that same woman is close enough to touch, to embrace . . . close enough for one to feel the heat of her body and smell its delicate aromas . . . when one can see oneself reflected in her bright, moist eyes – why then she is another creature altogether. My nether friend, my alter ego, agreed, for he began to hoist himself awake and press at the restraints of civilization.

"However," she continued, "flattering though your kind words about me were, they did, I fear reveal an astonishing ignorance of my true character and temperament. Believe me, it hurts me to say it, but I feel the matter is too important to leave in such an unsatisfactory state of misunderstanding. So I have come all the way to London, entirely on my own initiative (which I trust will commend me to you already), to tell you that, in whatever test you may wish to submit me, I am ready to stand." She lowered her voice and added, "Or sit or kneel or lie . . ."

I called out, "Thank you, Noakes, I can take care of this myself."

She embraced my arm and we went out together.

The cold air restored a little of my caution. "See here, Miss Bassington . . ." I began.

"Eve," she murmured.

"See here, Eve – I ought perhaps to tell you that I'm not going to Paris, Rome . . . all those places. In fact, you'd better know the brutal truth – the whole thing was just a confounded bet."

She considered this bombshell in silence and then came back, remarkably cheerfully: "What you say is naturally a great disappointment, Roger, my own, my very precious darling. However, I imagine your life, whether here or abroad, must be full of ups and downs. If we are not to stay at the Crillon in Paris, I suppose a sweet little villa in Maida Vale will complete my happiness just as well – especially if you are there for an hour or two each evening to solace me?"

I stopped and stared at her, for it was a most extraordinary thing. "How did you know I have a villa in Maida Vale? Good Lord! I'd even forgotten it myself. I haven't been there for ages."

"Dear me!" She was alarmed. "Has it . . . a present occupant? Have you perhaps forgotten her as well?"

I had to think. What the devil was the woman's name? Sarah? Susan? Yes – Susan! "Suzie Hanratty," I murmured. "No – I definitely saw her walking the Upper Circle at the Gaiety only last Monday. I *knew* there was something at the back of my mind when I spotted her. That was it – she walked out on me! I went out to have a jolly evening with her – at my villa in Maida Vale, indeed – last summer that was – and she'd packed up and gone. No wonder she beetled off so fast the other night."

"Well then, that is most satisfactory," Eve replied. "Are you going to take me there now? D'you have a cook, by the way? I hope so. I didn't dare go and eat on the train in case some colleague of my father's spotted *me*. One can't 'beetle off' too well on a train, can one?"

It was an extremely unfashionable hour for dining at the Café Royal so, being uncertain whether I still had a chef at Maida Vale, I thought it worth the risk of taking her there. We occupied a *chambre privée* up on the first floor. I forbear to record what quantities of food vanished down that sweetest and most delectable of throats; the train from the Wirral must have been three days in transit, that's all I can say. And meanwhile we talked.

The moment we were alone together, she moderated

her somewhat bantering tone and, fixing me with those adorable eyes, said, "I've staked everything on this, you know, Roger, my dear. I do hope it's going to work between us." She then went on to tell me a little about herself.

"I am, as I said - or perhaps I didn't - eighteen - unbetrothed and unattached. Last year, my father, thinking me lacking in some of my accomplishments, sent me as a companion to a wealthy lady, the sister of one of his business acquaintances. Good woman that she is, she hadn't the faintest suspicion in her head as to what was really going on in that household. Her husband had his hands up the skirts of everything that moved. A Scotchman of eighty with a full beard wouldn't have been safe. But he really set his sights on me."

"How awful for you," I commiserated.

"Not at all. I quite enjoyed it - not that I had the slightest intention of yielding to him, mind." She smiled at me. "Even then, utterly ignorant as I was in these matters, I suspected that my virginity had a certain value. Now I am sure of it - am I not right?"

I assured her she was, indeed.

"What are you going to offer me?" she asked - and then laughed and blushed. "No, no - don't answer yet. You don't know what you'd be buying."

She breathed in deeply - very deeply - thrusting into prominence at least part of the invoice, and then dispatched several mouthfuls before she went on. "I say I was not much affected by his importunity. It would be truer to say I took advantage of him. But fair's fair - it is what he wished to do of me. I told him I had no idea of what might be involved in the surrender of so precious a commodity. Of course, he offered at once to reveal every mystery of the entire business. I demurred and asked him if he could not first lend me some books on the subject – it was, I explained, a form of instruction to which I had been accustomed from my childhood. He lent me *Fanny Hill*. You probably know it?"

I said I had no doubt read it at some stage.

She nodded wistfully. "Yes, of course, with so much real experience you would find it most tame and forgettable. But I don't mind admitting – it has inflamed my desires until I hardly know how to hold myself in check."

"Yes, I recall that passage," I assured her.

She chuckled. "Well, the youngest son of the household, Tommy, also came at me whenever his father was occupied elsewhere . . . or do I mean occupy*ing* elsewhere?" She abandoned her quest for grammatical nicety when she saw me lift an anxious eyebrow; I, naturally, was more concerned with the content, rather than the form, of what she had just said. Then, smiling that bewitching smile yet again, she patted my hand. "Fear not, *darling* Roger, I have kept it all for you! Yes, indeed – for I had read your letter by then and was determined I should be your choice. So you may imagine my annoyance when you terminated the correspondence. However, young Tommy had his uses, for he lent me several more spicy tales. *The Romance of Lust* . . . I only ever finished Volume I of that – *Early Experiences*. But sufficient, I think. Also *Cythera's Hymnal,* subtitled *Flakes from the Foreskin*. I thought that was a trifle silly. The sort of book that simply glories in using dirty words. *Justine* by the Marquis de Sade was very distasteful – but it's useful to know such things go on. You're not like that, I hope?"

I shook my head and smiled. Actually, I was still trying to size her up. Girls who play "knowing" and "daring" like this are often more trouble than they are worth. If only she weren't so ravishingly beautiful!

"Good," she prattled on, "I was sure you weren't. I much preferred *L'Antijustine, ou les Délices de l'Amour,* which was written as a counter-blast."

"You have been a busy little scholar!"

"And an apt one, too – I hope." She bit her lower lip and raised her eyebrows, playing for a moment the naughty schoolgirl. Then she lowered her eyes demurely. "But that's what we're about to discover, isn't it, my dear. Is it in order now to discuss my price?"

I took her hands between mine and said, "If you become my mistress – even for one night – you will, for that period, be a courtesan of the very highest rank. I have, somewhere about my person (we shall discover it soon) an anointing rod that is charged with the capacity to ennoble the meanest slut. *You,* it will transform into a very princess of pleasure. But you should know that among such noble ladies it is well understood that money is never discussed. The cadeau that passes on completion of the transaction is so absurdly high that even the most mercenary of females would be embarrassed to discuss the matter at all."

She was a little tigress. She actually drew breath to dispute the point. I squeezed her hand even tighter. "If you wish to be told the precise sum," I murmured, "think of your dream, and then double it."

A small, nagging worry began to consume me. With almost every other female whose company and person I have enjoyed there has come a moment when an unmistakable resonance arose between us; most have been ladies of pleasure, of course, but it makes no difference. If a fine violin be played at a sympathetic pitch, then a suitably tuned crystal vessel will sing out in unison – and it will continue to vibrate when the bow is rested; it has no choice but to obey that law of nature. So it has been between me and the vast majority of women. I am that fine violin which can make the most jaded *grisette* suddenly open her eyes in astonishment, breathe deep, and sing out in a joy whose very existence she had long forgotten. She, too, can have no choice in the matter. I have seen it happen too often not to be aware of this power within me. But with my pretty little Eve, I was not so certain.

I blamed her choice of reading. Though still virgo intacta, she obviously believed her acquaintance with *Fanny Hill* had prepared her to be mounted and rodded without a qualm or surprise on her part. I could feel Mr Hardy down there, agreeing with my conclusion. He was absolutely chafing at the worsted, begging me to let him quench that babble, fill her with wonder, and astonish her into submission.

"Are you ready?" I asked, preparing to leave.

"No, I'd like some pudding," she said. "The *crême brulée,* I think. Our cook could never do that properly at home." She tucked into it as if it were her first dish of the evening. "Besides," she added, "I forgot to tell you what I'm offering. Even if we aren't to discuss my price, you should know what you'll be getting."

"I can bear the suspense," I assured her.

"But we have to do it properly. I can see it's a long time since you read any of those books. The heroines all begin by describing their own voluptuous charms. Or if the book is about a hero, he describes her from the point of view of the unquenchable lust she rouses within him. But, either way, one *must* start with The Description. You can begin with the bit about my face, if you like, because you can see it. I'll take over and tell you about my breasts, my waist, my delightful little *derrière,* and all my secret charms."

I could not suppress the smile that rose to my lips. This young lady was about to launch her frail and tender barque upon an ocean whose storms and tempests I had navigated for many years – and I am only twenty-seven. It was my simple duty to lift a small corner of but one of those myriad veils with which the Middle Classes like to obscure the subject.

"A beautiful woman," I told her, "seen across a crowded room, or even an uncrowded vestibule, is, as it were, no more than a picture, a vision – a remote and uncertain commodity. But as she draws near, there comes a point, an invisible line, where her effect on a man becomes devastating. In your case, darling Eve, I do not know where that line is. You devastated me from the moment I saw you. No conventional images will serve for you. Shall I call you angel, flower, rosebud . . .? For shame! There is in your face a haunting, almost alarming, perfection of feminine beauty that defies *all* description. And this is not because the lexicon of love is deficient but because my dumbfounded longing for you will not free me enough to reach for them. Yet you, who know nothing as yet, prattle so gaily of these terrifying forces. Do you truly suppose you can make yourself mistress of them in such a frivolous spirit?"

She stared at me, mouth agape. She had beautiful lips, made for so much more than kissing.

"Golly!" she murmured.

I let the silence return. "Yet – since you ask me to describe you, let me at least try. Of all those tired old words and phrases, the one that most nearly captures you is *flowerlike*. When I gaze at you, I see a rare beauty that can breathe new life into words like that. You may be as strong in spirit and as enduring as your namesake – old Eve herself; and yet there is a strange fragility about you, too. Your youth, your vivacity, your wayward charm – these have that sad-joyful allure of some rare orchid that dies at a touch. As I laugh and thrill to your sparkling youth, my eyes are pricked with tears for its very transience."

She gulped. I caressed her cheek; she gripped my hand and pressed it to her, closing her eyes and leaning into its touch.

"Were you about to tell me," I asked, letting my voice slowly harden, "of the supple trimness of your waist, the generosity of your breasts – ample but firm and with the most adorable pink buds for nipples? And your pert little bottom – so young and softly firm? And the delicate curve of your back as you thrust your *derrière* so invitingly toward me? The silken smoothness of your thighs, and the warm, dark, enticing folds of your Secret Smile? The . . ."

She gave a testy grunt – which is as close as anyone called Eve can get to an admission, I suppose.

I smiled. "Then your reading has taught you nothing. Believe me, the wonder we are about to discover between us does not reside in such anatomical marvels. The fat old frow of four and fifty can crack and rejoice at that same flame with a bald old skinshanks of a man ten years her senior. The pleasure I am about to take between your thighs – and the pleasure you are about to feel as you spread them to me – is the profoundest mystery of all, beside which the riddle of the Sphinx is but a child's rebus. It is a mystery in which all that is feminine in you must strive against all that is masculine in me – and yet strive *with* it, too, in an endless quest for raptures that will always *just* elude us. Think of poor Adam – your first husband – alone in Eden. Poor Adam, who had never even seen a woman, nor feasted his gaze on female flesh, nor plumbed the pools of a young maid's eyes . . . poor Adam nonetheless knew her very name: *Woman!* Poor

Adam knew what he lacked; poor Adam knew he must ask God to create her - and poor, poor Adam knew in his heart that it would cost them both - him and her - their very tenure in Paradise. Yet he faltered not for half a syllable!' I patted her hand reassuringly. "And out of the depths of that same mystery - tonight - you and I shall raise up a pleasure that will help us understand *why!* Why they risked all, lost all. We shall rediscover the gains that outweighed even so monstrous a loss - and have done so for his and her descendants to this day. But even more than that, my dearest Eve, we shall discover why an all-wise and all-loving God allowed them to take that step toward their own damnation."

She touched my cheek tenderly. "How beautiful," she murmured. "Would it be terrible of me to ask for another helping of the *crême brulée?"*

It was a deliberate provocation, of course; but I was not annoyed. I have a penchant for a mettlesome filly. Fifteen minutes later we were in a hansom and bound for my villa in Maida Vale.

That same "kind and loving God" also has a vicious sense of humour. My servants at the villa, long used to my forgetful absence, had locked up and gone off dancing for the night. We had to return to the Albany to get my own key. By then, naturally, the mood I had so carefully built up between us, was entirely dissipated.

But worse was to follow.

When we arrived at the Albany there was a buxom, rather plain young girl waiting by the porter's lodge. "Here's Number Two, my lord," he said with roguish deference. "Miss Wilhelmina Clark of Gloucester."

Miss Clark showed considerably more economy of effort - and even more presence of mind - than had Miss Bassington. Miss Clark stood up, offered me her hand, and fainted. I should have been the laughing stock of London for weeks if anyone had come in at that moment; she left me no choice but to take her with us. Also, to be sure, I was moved by a certain compassion. She had the look of a girl who deserved more from life than life had so far served her. And who better to provide it than I?

"Too much water, not enough wine," I explained to the pair of policemen who helped me get her into our growler.

When we passed them a minute or so later, they were still arguing over whether I had said what they thought I said. Eve laughed with a guarded sort of impetuosity; I have often noted that a woman gives her body as she gives her laughter. "What are you going to do with her?" she asked as we turned into Regent Street.

"She appears to have applied for the same position as you," I pointed out. "It would be only fair to give her the same chance at it."

"But . . . you can't. I mean – she's fat and . . . well, not to mince words, rather plain."

I smiled. "If I *prick* her, will she not *bleed?"*

Miss Bassington became thoughtful after that, and managed to remain so all the way to Maida Vale. I hoped she was reflecting that it was she, not I, who had made it a commodity and she who had tried to fix its price.

The next-door servants must have gone down to the dance hall and alerted mine, for when we came back the house was ablaze with light, fires were kindled and burning, and the air was drowsy with incense. They protested we could not have knocked loud enough. We allowed them to preserve that fiction until after breakfast the following morning, when they were all dismissed without characters.

Miss Clark, who recovered consciousness on the journey, was still drowsy and unwell when we arrived. She refused all offers of food but accepted some Vichy water. Before she drank, she raised the glass toward me as a kind of toast; the gesture was almost conspiratorial.

"Fat and plain," was a cruel description of her because there was just enough truth in it to hurt – certainly as far as "plain" went. Her face was not pretty, I had to admit as I took my first opportunity to examine her closely; it was rather square, dominated by a broad nose and a determined jaw. Her eyes, however, if one mentally masked off the rest, smouldered with a reserved and watchful passion; by candlelight, as I later saw upstairs, they even acquired a strangely haunting beauty. "Fat," however, was simply not true; she was broad, she was short, she was amply fleshed, but, or so I guessed, it was all firm and strong. It was a guess I intended to confirm at the earliest opportunity; for the moment I settled for "buxom." I took her to my dressing room and told her she might sleep there undisturbed until morning – when we should sit down together and have a jolly chinwag about her future.

"And now?" Eve asked when we were alone at last. "A bath, I presume? You have some perfume?"

"No," I told her. "I want you just as you are." I turned her away from me and began unhooking the bodice of her dress.

I seem to have gone off at a sort of literary half-cock – a verbal premature ejaculation, i.e., got too far ahead in my story. The fact is, to understand the Sentimental Education of those two delightful young fillies, you must first know something of mine. I think you will agree that two more fortunate girls never drew breath and that Casanova himself could not have made a finer teacher.

The first erotic experience I can remember was at the age of five. I went out early one morning to pick mushrooms and found Becky Hythe, one of the gardeners' daughters, a girl of ten, at the same pastime. The sun was well up as we set off for home and she stopped to relieve herself in a ditch. Her manner of squatting down and the fact that the golden stream poured out backwards fascinated me, as did the strange folds of flesh that I glimpsed between her thighs.

"Here's how *I* do it," I boasted, in the manner of all little boys of five. But, although I produced Wee Willie Winkie proudly enough, some unaccountable shyness prevented him from performing.

"D'you know what the big boys and girls do?" she asked.

I, of course, said yes, though I really hadn't the first idea.

"Good," she went on. "Come and look at this, then."

It was many years before I realized that if I had said no, she would have protected me from what followed – she would have taken me directly home; she did not want to be the first to show me the Great God Pan, if only by proxy.

Our proxies on that day were the foreman of our home farm, a man called Mangolees, and a pauper girl from a field gang hired out by the workhouse. She was about seventeen and very comely. He was about fifty and a veteran of hundreds of such encounters – which blunted the sharp edge of his desire and made him a better lover of women than many a younger man. To me, of course, a woman of seventeen and a man of fifty were both "grown ups," and seemed much of an age.

Experienced whores prefer young men because they rouse quickly, shoot quickly, and let them get back to the street (and the next fee-paying customer) in double-quick time. But a loving woman is almost always disappointed in them. Women are slow to fire and burn with a deeper, more passionate flame. A lover who takes his time, who enjoys giving her pleasure as much as taking his own, beats impetuous youth into the ha'penny position. Bill Mangolees was such a lover. Years later, when scandal of his doings leaked out, not a single pauper girl, past or present, could be found to bear witness against him – there you have the measure of the man!

And on that day, the measure of the man was what this comely wench from the workhouse was getting, in full. She had taken her skirt off and he his breeches. Her shirt was open and her ample breasts spilled down over her corsets. She lay on her back with the leg nearest us thrown up over his posteriors; and in that position she was guiding him in and out to her rhythm, for I could clearly see the muscles and sinews in the back of her upstretched thigh tightening and slackening in time with his movements.

Becky and I lay in the long grass at the edge of the glade, not six paces from them, so we could see everything, every little fold or her flesh, every wrinkle on his balls, every hair. As an erotic experience it meant nothing to me at that age, of course; I mean, I had no erotic feelings myself, no erection, no tingling in Willie Winkie. And yet I was held in utter fascination by what I saw.

And so it was with Becky, too, though she was older. Knowing what I now know of female lust, I believe she would have tried *something* with me if she herself had been stirred. Friends at Eton told me of the most hair-raising things they and their sisters, and the sisters' friends, got up to around the age of ten; and though I know a lot of it was pure boasting, I'm sure there was a residue of actual carnality in it. Yet Becky and I watched on an innocent as babes.

It was clear to us that Mangolees and his lass were deriving the most enormous pleasure from this strange activity. Their sighs rose in pitch and intensity like the notes of a skylark. At last they grew so wild they began to embarrass us. I myself was greatly excited by it, not in a sexual way, but just generally caught up in it. I was also embarrassed at feeling like that and began to giggle. Becky panicked at once and dragged me out of the covert, back into the field. Then, laughing like mad things, we ran all the way home.

After that I often sneaked out alone when I thought I might catch Mangolees and one of the pauper girls "at it". Sometimes I found Becky there, more often not. Although I had no awareness of sex, I knew that what they were doing was somehow wrong; and I think it was an awareness of their wrongdoing that fascinated me. If they had been a pair of burglars breaking into a house and I could have watched, it would have been with the same terrified fascination.

And yet who can tell what really goes on in the mind of a lad of five, or six, or seven? For those were the years in which, I spied on Mangolees and his maid of the moment, perhaps half a dozen times each year. I must confess that when I later became an *active* devotee of the same four-legged frolic, the things I had watched him do had already become a natural part of my own repertoire. I never rushed into a woman unless she was already as wet as Niagara when I got my fingers to her cleft. I knew, as if the knowledge were innate, that a variation of rhythm and depth will drive one woman wild while another may crave a rock-steady pace and a thrust to the hilt each time. I knew that the woman who wants variations one day will yearn for uniformity on another. All this and much, much more I believe I learned from my alfresco tutors – none of whom, I'm sure, even knew of my existence!

My next conscious memory of Venus is from the time when I was about ten or eleven, when my aunt, the Countess of Clanbrasil, came to visit. She had a very lively reputation in her youth and I suppose something of it must have filtered down into the nursery, where vast amounts of knowledge rest on the most fleeting gestures, half-spoken sentences, hastily suppressed smiles. It all came about because my younger brother and I had the habit of larking about under the table at dinner. Our favourite trick was to creep in unobserved (or so we thought – in fact, we had the world's most tolerant parents). Then we would crawl up and down in the gloom beneath the tablecloth, trying to guess which feet belonged to whom, and sometimes tying their shoelaces together. They, for their part, would say things like, "Someone's let the beastly dogs in here . . . I say, what a bore . . . give them a thorough kick!"

One day we crept in before the grown-ups arrived, determined to see how long we could stay under the table without being noticed. *That* was a revelation, I may say! I have never been able to sit at a public dinner since without wondering if all those solemn ladies and gentlemen, talking to each other with such gravity, or listening to a speaker with the most serious mien, are not actually in the wildest throes of sexual revelry beneath those samite tablecloths.

My aunt, whom I now realize was a very pretty thirty-six but who seemed as old as the auk then, was the most scandalous of all. She wore the usual sort of dress of the period – a bustle and two or three petticoats beneath a silk skirt that fell almost sheer in front. Crinolines had been gone for years by then. On that particular evening, my bro and I crawled slowly up the centre line of the table, which was ten feet wide, so we were in little danger of accidental discovery by a carelessly placed foot. As we went we whispered to each other, "Uncle Osbert . . . Aunt Horatia . . . Lady Fausse-Delauney . . ." and so on. We went by the dress material for the women, of course, for there was nothing else to see – until we came to my aunt, the Countess. We were almost shocked out of our wits to discover a white rainbow of frilly lace draped over two extremely shapely legs encased in sheer *purple* silk stockings; it was like going through some worthy library full of improving literature and suddenly coming across one of the ballerina magas that the fellows used to pass around at school. She was actually in the act of rolling this rainbow farther up her thighs as we arrived – not in one continuous movement, to be sure, for that would have attracted notice above the tablecloth.

All this while she was telling a story about a hunt in Ireland that had gone disastrously and hilariously wrong. Whenever the company laughed, which was fairly often, her hand would casually drop to her lap and then sneak down her thigh to the present limit of her skirt, which it would then roll up a further inch or two. My bro and I were old enough by then to know that there was something rather funny about that part of the human anatomy which lies between wind and water. Most of our jokes and conversation, indeed, were about those very functions and we had not yet sorted them out from the ways of venery itself. So we sat in high glee to watch whatever naughtiness might be in train.

We had not long to wait. Soon her thighs were fully exposed – but only her thighs. That is, she kept her knees together very demurely as yet. She then gave a surreptitious dig with her elbow to the gentleman at her left, my Uncle Demetrius, the husband of one of Clanbrasil's female cousins. He waited about half a minute and then allowed his hand to fall to his lap. A moment later it began to snake over toward her exposed limbs. She, meanwhile, went on with her tale of the hunt. Her voice did not even falter when his hand at last arrived at its immediate goal.

In the circumstances he could make no violent motion so all his caresses were languorous and slow, from about half way down her thigh up to her fork, which was still nestling in the dark under the frills of her dress. If limbs could speak hers would have sighed. Slowly, under the relentless pressure of that tormenting hand, they *sighed* themselves apart and offered everything they had so far concealed to his importunate exploration.

All unknowing, the same gesture also offered us two young scamps the most perfect view of Old Mossyface we had ever seen. There was a schoolboy joke current at the time: *Q: Have you seen Mars? A: No, but I've seen pa's and it's huge!* It had always made me wonder what "ma's" was like, really close-to. I had, to be sure, seen many a glimpse of the Holey of Holeys, thanks to Mangolees and his pauper totties; but I had never been granted a close-to vision of paradise like that. It was a bright summer evening, so nothing was lost in impenetrable gloom. Naturally, I went forward, as near as I could, to satisfy my curiosity.

I was not the only one. My uncle's fingers were satisfying more than his curiosity, to judge by the glistening wetness of my aunt's treasure (I say all this with benefit of hindsight, of course). As if for my instruction they worked tenderly up and down in that honeyed morass of her flesh, parting its oysterlike folds, showing me its delightful secrets one by one. Actually, I think I am more excited now in recalling it than I was at the time. I was still not old enough for anything but my curiosity to be excited by what I saw; indeed, I remember an acute sense of disappointment that I had not been able to see her bumhole. What a trophy that would have been to an eleven-year-old scallywag like me! We only had to say the word "bum" to dissolve in hysterics. To have got so close to that revelation and yet be denied the victory was a bitter blow. Ah, what happy innocence!

My next step along the path to sexual enlightenment came a year or so later, when I was about twelve. There were other additions to the nursery and I was sent to sleep in a room with two servant girls – ladies' maids, of course . . . girls of fairly good class. As I write of it now I am amazed at my parents' innocence – especially when I have good reason to know that my father suffers from the "Irish toothache" almost as severely as do I; but it was a large, attic room and my bed was well away from theirs and divided from it by a heavy velvet curtain. All of which must have reassured them. Besides, the two maids were, as I say, of a good class.

Their names were Marian and Lizzie. Marian was small, slender, and dark; Lizzie had fair, honey-coloured hair and was altogether more buxom. For the first few nights I was aware that they were lying there, seething with resentment, for they could no longer chatter away and gossip about us – the masters. Also, as I was soon to learn, they liked to pleasure each other before going off to sleep, and my presence put a stop to all that.

However, after a few nights the temptation of lying side by side in their big double bed overcame them and, when they thought I was asleep (a delusion to which my deep, slow, regular breathing may have contributed), they began their gentle work upon each other's bodies. By now I had some idea what they might be doing, so, maintaining the noisy respirations they took for my slumber, I crept from the bed, parted the curtain by the tiniest crack, and had a good, bold look at them. It was disappointing. All I could see was heaving bedclothes – and the room was pretty dark at that. The sighing and moaning kept me glued to my post, however.

After a while their passion heated them up and they began to throw off their coverings, first the eiderdown, then the blankets. The sheets they kept over them, but, being both white and thin, they revealed a great deal more, though most of it was still left to my imagination to (as it were) flesh out.

Still being a most ignorant voyeur, I could not really imagine what they were doing to each other; surely neither of them was equipped to play the role of Mangolees? They would take it in turns to vanish below the sheet and, from the movement of the resulting lumps, it was quite clear that the girl whose head I could see was lying on her back with her knees bent and thighs parted wide; the hidden girl was on all fours with her head nestled in the other's crotch. The visible girl would gasp and writhe with pleasure at this. Sometimes she would reach up and grab the iron crossbar of the brass bedstead, pulling herself right off the bed and lifting her treasure higher into the other's kiss . . . or whatever it was (I had no idea then). At other times she would caress her own breasts, throwing down the sheet to give them air.

This they did three or four times each week. It was

several weeks before they became aware that I was, in fact, watching all they did. There was no actual moment of shocked discovery; and not a word on the subject passed between us. They simply because aware that I was watching and, some weeks later still, I became aware that they knew. By then I no longer bothered to feign sleep – though I did nothing to show that I was wide awake, either. My bed, too, I had moved to lie alongside the curtain, and under my pillow I kept a short piece of kindling wood, about six inches long and sharpened at each end, to hold the gap in the curtains apart. Thus I could lie comfortably on my side, snuggled into the bedclothes, and watch them at my ease. They, for their part, "forgot" to blow out the lamp until their frolics were over!

Some years later, in circumstances I am about to relate, they told me they enjoyed knowing I was their audience. It had made their revels all the more piquant. I had some intimation of this at the time, to be sure, from the way they cast aside all the bedclothing, when the nights were not too cold, and permitted me an uninterrupted ringside view of all their doings. They usually required about forty minutes for their pleasure to turn to satiety. In that time they squirmed and wriggled all over each other, face to face and soixante-neuf; they licked, caressed, kissed, and sucked; they fingered and used candles; they sighed and moaned and gasped; they thrashed their legs and shivered and lay rigid and strained and collapsed into utter openness and vulnerability.

And I watched.

For four long years I watched. During the last two of those years, between the ages of fourteen and sixteen, I was at Eton and only enjoyed that privilege during the vacations. By then, like all boys of that age, I had learned to get myself off, which I did four or five times during the girls' exhibitions. Knowing myself as I do now, it is utterly beyond my comprehension that I never once made a move to go beyond that curtain and join them. Knowing them, as I did later, it is also amazing that they made no move to invite me. I suppose we had fallen into a pattern and it was so enjoyable and familiar we did not wish to risk breaking it.

And if my parents had not suddenly woken up to the fact that I was still - at sixteen - sleeping in the maids' room, we might well have stuck to that same pattern until I went up to 'varsity! But, in their wisdom, my father and mother decided I should be moved out into a virtuous room of my own - and then the fat *was* in the fire.

How I pined for Marian and Lizzie! My fevered dreams were laced with images of their lovely young bodies, twined together, pleasuring each other for all they were worth. I used to imagine I could hear their gasps and moans, carrying through the still, dark corridors, taunting me. Inciting me. Enticing me. Inviting me!

At last, after several days of that deprivation, I could endure it no longer. I crept through the labyrinth of the house, honing that instinct for a loose floorboard or a creaking wainscote which later saved my bacon more than once. Through the green baize door I went, and up to the large attic bedroom where I had known so much joy. I did not knock. I merely slipped into their room, and listened. My practised ear informed me they had just begun. The lip-smacking noises and the gentle, "Mmmms" and "Aaahs" meant they were lying side by side, kissing each other's cheeks and necks and caressing each other's bodies. They would be naked by now, too.

I glided like a ghost across the floor, shedding my

nightshirt as I went. Then I lifted their bedclothes, and slipped in between them. I was, of course, chilled from my walk; they were like two spicy furnaces.

Now, what do you suppose happened next, eh?

Well, yes, of course *that* happened. But how did we get to it? What lay between their surprised cries at my sudden appearance between them and my losing my virginity (and taking theirs with it, as things turned out)? Laughter? Explanations? Whispered dares? Pleadings from me and modest refusals from them, which turned to gradual acceptance? "You go first, Marian," "No! *You,* Lizzie."?

It is certainly what *I* expected. It is what I had prepared myself to go through. But in fact, just as we had never spoken a word about our mutual connivance at their exhibitionism and my voyeurism over the past four years, so now, not a word did we say concerning this new development. Later, to be sure, we couldn't *stop* talking of it. But at that all-important moment when I slipped my chill bones between their hot, voluptuous bodies, we simply began the mutual enjoyment of each other as if it had been arranged so for weeks.

My years of unconscious learning from old Mangolees, a seasoned and considerate lover of women, followed by my intimate observation of the caresses and tricks in which these two nymphs had revelled, now came to buoy me up. I have since heard other chaps confess what giddy asses they made of themselves on their "first time", which I can readily credit. So I now know how fortunate I was in my years of happy voyeuristic tutelage. One fellow at the club, Bunty Hawthornden, told me he'd "always sort-of known that women are docked smack-smooth down there and sort-of went in slightly, somewhere in the heart of that bit they left out on all the statues." But when he poked himself vaguely at it, he was still astounded to find that the rumours were quite true! And a moment later he was squirting off all over the place. What the opinion of his partner might have been at such a lamentable performance he did not say.

For an hour or so I passed between Marian and Lizzie, our vigorous young bodies *gorging* upon one another in every possible attitude and with every variation in pace and depth of penetration. At last, when they were sated with pleasure and the thrills of orgasm were beginning to shade into pain, they begged me to finish and let them sleep. Now, there were quite a few experienced men at Eton, and from them I had learned that a gentleman would never embarrass a lady by finishing in her baby-making hole. So, being deep into Lizzie at the time, I whipped the Lad out of her well of delights and pushed him firmly into her bumhole, where a few swift pokes brimmed him over.

I already knew Lizzie was sensitive in that particular socket for I had often seen Marian wriggling her little finger there while, at the tame time, rodding her proper hole with a candle *and* suckling her *cocquille de joie*. But even her most violent threshings under the sweetness of that triple torture had not prepared me for the explosion of pleasure she now enjoyed. Weeks later, when we first began speaking of it in our shy way, she told me that feeling my good friend inside her there, pouring his heart out with such leaps of joy, had been like "visiting all four corners of the world in one go."

Marian was so disappointed that Lizzie had been favoured with the first anointing that she burst into tears. But the Lad was even more game then than he is now; and another five minutes of vigorous poking in that same safe retreat (where she, too, was exquisitely sensitized) brought the blessed quietus her body had craved. The pleasure of it was so intense she passed out. I left my two sweet nymphs cuddling each other in their exhaustion and did the Dead March from *Saul* back to my virtuous bed in my own virtuous room in the virtuous part of the house.

Looking back on it now, I can feel grateful to my three wonderful mentors in the University of Pleasure: Mangolees, Marian, and Lizzie. And, to be sure, young Becky, the gardener's daughter, whose little-girlish curiosity had started it all. And I am glad, too, that I did not "jump the gun" with either of those two nymphs. I'm sure that my precocious manhood would have been *up to it* as far as mere physical performance goes. But, as any man or woman will tell you after their first hundred or so pokes, mere physical performance is the least part of true pleasure. However, I did not know that then, and I wasted hours in cursing myself for my timidity and pusillanimity and cowardice . . . I raked the lexicon for scourges to my own back.

Marian and Lizzie became exhausted if we indulged in our aphrodisiac romps more than twice a week, though I could have gone hard at them every night and twice on Sundays; so I had plenty of time for those solitary pleasures and fantasies that fill out the hours between waking and sleep in the life of every lusty young lad. And all my fantasies were that I had, indeed, leaped upon little Becky and enjoyed her to the last dry squirt.

I can laugh now, but it became a powerful and compelling image in my erotic imagination at that time. I made her a little older than she had been. In fact, I put her at twelve, which, as all we big, bold lads at Eton knew, was the age at which a girl becomes legally fair game. [*Actually, Hornington was wrong. The Criminal Law Amendment Act of 1880 raised the*

32

age of consent for a girl to thirteen! FR.] I liked to imagine her lying on her back with her legs in the air, wide open, while I lay between them and gazed in adoration at her light, downy lips and pushed an exploring finger into her unvisited hole. Then I would wriggle up her belly and push Wee Willy Winkie into that warm, tight, slippery passage and jiggle away until I got tired. Now it makes me laugh; but then I could spend just thinking about it.

I also used to imagine that, instead of just watching my two nymphs through the curtain all the years I slept in their room, I had slipped from my bed and joined them. Then, of course, being twelve or so, I gave a better account of myself. We ran away to Robinson Crusoe islands or stumbled upon Oriental hareems, mysteriously untenanted (plague, or something, but we were vaccinated), and there we enjoyed impossible week-long orgies of sensual pleasure. In my shame at my timidity, I invented an erotic pedigree of which any man might be proud.

One night, after I had been going to the girls for about a year, I had just begun the pleasurable night-crawl to their bedroom, when I came upon my aunt, the Countess of Clanbrasil. She, I realized, was at the same game, probably with Uncle Demetrius, who was also visiting us at that time. She immediately pretended she was going to the earth closet at the end of the corridor; she even assured me, with the sweetest smile, that she wouldn't be long. With a cocky grin I told her I was sorry to hear it. *I* could make it last an hour for her if she preferred – adding that I also wouldn't expect her to come night-crawling to me. She was too shocked to reply.

But she must have had a word with my father because the following week, three days before my seventeenth birthday, he came to me and said,

"Speaking for myself, young Roger my boy, I feel this may be rather premature. But my sister assures me it ain't. I had to wait till my eighteenth birthday, at which time my pater took me to a house in Paris and gave me the pick of the girls. I chose a bright-eyed little blonde filly, led her upstairs, and rode her all night. When I awoke, my innocence was nowhere to be seen. Well, there's no chance of Paris for you, I fear, but there's plenty of totties hereabout who could do as well. They're all warm and wet in the dark – so, what's your fancy?"

I thanked him profoundly and said I felt that any girl older than me might be rather intimidating – which was true. When I had left my aunt after making that vain and boastful offer, I came over all a-tremble and thanked my stars she had not accepted. I had never imagined myself in the arms of an older and more experienced woman. I was not mentally prepared for it. True, both Marian and Lizzie were six or seven years my senior, but they had grown up evenly in experience with me. And, during each half at Eton, the little village doxies who had spread their legs to me for a few shillings were in no true sense "professionals." So I said if he could find a girl born on the same day as me, who would be willing for us to spend the night of our common birthday together, he could not give me a better present.

Jenny was her name – a shy young thing with long, flaming red hair and the gaze and nerviness of a wild fawn. She was my height all but half an inch, slender, willowy, and exceedingly graceful in her movements. She looked as if one good ride with Captain Standish would exhaust her, but my father (surely the best in all the world) had assured me she was already well gone in experience. Her speech was most respectable, so either her powers of mimicry or her origins were good.

She, however, was nowhere near so happy with her assignment. I have often noticed since that the younger whores are happiest with elderly men. The idea of initiating one their own age would not appeal to many among them. A more experienced woman in her twenties, however, would find such a commission highly piquant.

Jenny asked a trifle airily what experience I had had with girls or women. I thought it best to say I had had little. She sighed and asked me if I knew the differences between us. "Oh yes," I said. "Down here you are made to receive me. But I have never seen it – except what may be guessed from paintings and statues – and would so dearly love to gaze upon it, for everyone says it is the most beautiful thing."

"Well, then you may." She laughed, relaxing a little to discover I was neither the pimply, ungainly youth she had feared to meet nor tongue-tied and bashful, either.

She sat on the edge of the bed, lay back on her elbows, and invited me to lift her skirts and gaze upon her secret treasure to my heart's content. Trembling with desire, I began to fold back what seemed like an acre of frothy, creamy frills. Her shapely young legs were encased in silk stockings, so smooth and warm I could not stop myself from bending to kiss them. "You will permit it?" I asked.

"Tonight, my darling Roger, I will permit you anything. My body is yours to discover and explore. Use it as you will for your pleasure. You owe me nothing but your own delight in me."

Thus she revealed to me the difference between a whore and even the most experienced and willing of amateur – or amateuse – sleeping partners. With the amateuse one borrows, so to speak, the use of her body and one must treat her as one would, say, a borrowed villa; one feels only a conditional sort of welcome, and, no matter how often and how sincerely the lender might encourage one to "make yourself at home" and "treat the place as your own", that sort of easy usage lies forever beyond one. But a whore offers, as it were, a leasehold - for an hour or a night rather than for a year or a life, but no matter; during the term of the lease the property is ours to use at our absolute ease. For example, with the amateuse it is almost *de rigeur* to fondle her breasts and start her spinning before turning one's attention to her honeyed cleft, which is where I always longed to begin - as, indeed, I did in my fantasies with young Becky. With Jenny, there was no need for the detour.

But it went deeper than that. One of my favourite pastimes with my two delightful maids was to press my upper lips to their nether ones and kiss and lick until I grew drunk on that nectar which begins to flow when girls are roused to their pleasure. But, passionate as they were, when that arousal began to stir their bellies, my darlings would close their thighs upon me and wriggle themselves down between the sheets, hauling me up until our heads were level, whereupon they would sigh such things as, "Quick, my love, go in, go in, and ride me hard for all you're worth." Once or twice I managed to pleasure Lizzie, always the more curious of the two, all the way to her private paradise, using only my tongue and lips; but she was too conventional a lass at heart and said it "didn't feel right, somehow, going pop without a bit of gristle hard inside her." They could do it for hours with each other, but when there was a real man there with a hard creamstick ready to overflow, their patience just shrivelled.

But now, with Jenny's mercenary consent to anything and everything, I could gorge myself until *I* was sated.

And so I now intended to do.

Above her silk stockings was a pair of lace drawers of amazing complexity; they encased the upper halves of her slender thighs in frills and tucks that would have inflamed the dullest of men. At each side of her centre of bliss were fine slits in the material, through which I could glimpse the pink of her flesh and the pale ginger of her hair. These drawers were much shorter than usual, the waistband being at the level of her hips, an inch or two beneath her navel - as I discovered with the final roll of her skirts, exposing all her delightfully nude belly.

I asked her to spread her thighs well apart and then assume as comfortable a position as she could, for I considered I might be at her fork for some time. She eased herself farther onto the bed and lay fully back. I placed a pillow beneath her head, for which she smiled up at me gratefully. "Is all as you expected so far?" she asked kindly.

"Oh, it is a dream coming true," I told her.

She laughed. "A great deal more than that will be coming in a while," she promised. Then she wriggled luxuriously and urged me not to hurry as we had all night for our pleasure. I placed a second pillow on the floor for my knees and returned to my ecstatic contemplation of her as yet concealed charms. The wider parting of her limbs had opened those slits in her drawers to a width of almost an inch, through which I could see the fine creases of her flesh between her outer lips and their junction with her thighs - as well as the delicate little curls of bright red hair that adorned them. Also my nostrils were filled with that most aphrodisiac aroma in the whole universe - I mean the civet which emanates from the sexual glands of a redheaded girl. I thought I should swoon when first it assailed me.

The parting in the garment ran all the way up to the waistband. I slipped my tremulous fingers beneath that covering to caress the fine downy skin above her mound of Venus – in small, circular movements, ending where her bosky fur began. "Don't be bashful," she murmured, "move your fingers on down. D'you feel that cleft? That's it. That's the beginning of the way into paradise. Now run your finger on down there and see what it discovers for you – only gently, mind. We are very tender there."

Of course, I knew very well what I should find but I pretended ignorance and when I discovered her little pearl of rapture I caressed it in the way that used to drive my maids frantic and said, "Oh, and pray what is that?"

Her thighs had a sudden, tiny spasm and she said, slightly breathless, "That is a *most* tender part. Go lower. There! Now that is not my holey of holeys. It is my planter of sweet peas. Go on just a little – yes! There!"

I gulped. "Is that *it?*"

"Yes, my darling. That is love's Grand Canal to heaven, where you shall navigate tonight. Feel how snug and warm and juicy she is, my dainty little honeypot. Go one – right in – all the way . . .'

"I can't," I gasped. "Your drawers are in the way."

Her nimble fingers crept down over the roll of her skirt and undid several small hooks, revealing that the central portion of her drawers was but a flap. And oh, what treasure its falling away revealed! Even now, when I can truthfully claim to have gazed at a thousand and more of those sweet, adorable little mossyfaces,

I remember it as one of the most perfect I ever saw, exquisite and fine, with a sheen on her flesh like mother of pearl. Her outer lips, which were smooth and downy, parted softy to reveal the more complex and sinuous folds of her inner pair, which gleamed and furled in the most voluptuous way, spreading a little over her rosebud and puckering tenderly around her portals of paradise.

"They look so like lips," I said, "may I not kiss them, please?"

She giggled. "But of course."

I kissed them, I suckled them, I licked, I writhed my tongue over them this way and that . . . I teased her gently pouting oyster with a mouth that was never still. She rose to a pleasure she did not welcome, for she wished to remain in control and – subtly – to dictate what we might do. I felt her beginning to squirm away from me, just as Marian and Lizzie used to.

"No, please?" I begged, rising and lifting her thighs from their relaxed V only to pin them to the bed almost level with her hips, so that they were spread as wide as is physically possible. Then I fell back on that gleaming young fig of hers and devoured it. She twitched and jolted with that same unwilling rapture. She writhed in vain beneath my weight. Her fists rose and fell upon the counterpane. He head tossed wildly from side to side, throwing her hair into disarray. The sweat started out all over her.

"Mercy!" she begged at last.

I relented and pulled down her dress and threw myself on the bed beside her, panting with as much desperation as she – though in my case it was from a delirious suffocation at the pit of all joys.

"You *have* been with a girl before," she accused as her self-possession returned.

"Snatched fumblings with servant girls," I assured

her. "I thought you would laugh at me if I mentioned them."

She was still panting quite hard. "Well, my darling, you may do what you like with me now. I assure you I shall not laugh. No man – not even those most sunk in lechery – has ever gone at me so long nor so skilfully down there." She smiled delightfully. "What next? Or d'you want me to suggest something?"

I took off her dress and bodice but left on all her underthings; then I laid her on her back and parted her thighs by kneeling between them – where I stripped myself to my shirt and trousers. As I removed my waistcoat her lively little fingers made short work of my flies.

"Goodness," she exclaimed on seeing my desperate erection, hot from desire and pulsing with impatience.

There were lamps and candles all around the bed but I turned her slightly to where the brightest light fell on her fork. Then I lifted her to me, keeping her raised by slipping my thighs beneath the backs of hers, and then, bearing down on my urgent fellow, got the tip of him inside her. She gave a little cry of joy, closed her eyes, and lay there, utterly passive, her lips parted in a lascivious smile. It boosted my self-confidence to the skies, for, in effect, she was saying. "Now I leave it all to you."

There was surely some strange communion of desire between us from that moment on. I measured her insides in every possible way without changing her position on her back beneath me. After some twenty minutes, during which she thrilled again, I felt my loins gathering to spend. I whipped the fellow out of her, spun her over, and went hard into Brownhaven, spending almost immediately.

She gasped with an astonishment that swiftly brimmed over into delight; our cries of ecstasy raised several amused and envious brows in my father's household I was later told.

"Why did you do that?" she asked when we had recovered ourselves somewhat. In fact, we were standing at the hand basin washing her fork and the Lad.

"So as not to embarrass you," I explained. "Nine months from now."

"Oh, bless you!" She laughed and kissed me tenderly. "You're not to worry about that! We take precautions, you know." After a pause she added, "D'you realize your creamstick down here is still hard?"

'Naturally. He hasn't finished with you yet."

She grinned and asked what he wanted next.

I led her to one of the long mirrors and, standing behind her, took off her chemise, thus gaining my first unimpeded view of her two adorable breasts. If I was well endowed for a youth my age, then so was she. They were full and firm, with large, conical nipples that swelled desperately at my touch. She gave out a little whimper, closed her eyes, and raised her lips to mine. "I don't know what you've done to me," she whispered. "There'll be neither teaching nor learning tonight, my darling - and precious little whoring, either."

"Eh?" I asked, for at that time I did not realize how few men are able to please a whore - nor how few whores are willing to let them.

But she would not explain. She turned and took off my shirt, running her dainty fingers over my chest and caressing and suckling my nipples - which has as great an effect on me as it does on any woman. The Lad was again rampant to be at her. She led me to the bed and laid me on my back; there, while easing off my trousers, she slipped her mouth around the knob of him and almost took the scalp off me with the pleasures she could give. I have known many a good suckstress since but the best of them was no more than equal to my darling young Jenny that night.

This time she rode me – the St George's gallop, as they call it, except that she saw it in more satanic terms. "I am the she-devil on your broomstick," she said, with her lovely breasts swinging inches from my face. And when I rose to my climax she sat into me like a huntsman gathering his steed for a leap, and so I leaped up into her and felt my spending flying like pellets of shot in the deepest recesses of her belly, while she collapsed upon me, sighing and moaning in an equal joy.

Then we lay awhile and talked. She told me she was the daughter of a wealthy merchant who had failed when she was fifteen, almost sixteen. She had overheard one of her father's creditors offering to let him off the largest part of his total debt in return for the enjoyment of her virginity – which her father would not even contemplate. She had then gone secretly to the man – having only the vaguest idea of what he might desire – and concluded the bargain, actually on her sixteenth birthday.

"I seem to be lucky with my birthdays," she said with a smile.

I asked what she meant by that and she explained.

In a book of moral fables that man who deflowered her would have been a brute who left her torn and bleeding; in truth he was a gentle, considerate man who took three nights of careful and tender encouragement to bring her to her sacrifice. She had felt no pleasure that first time with him – yet no pain to speak of, either; by morning, however, she had seen the Great God Pan. Her parents, torn between disgust and heartbreak, would not have her back. She had remained her seducer's mistress for several months before he passed her on to the Duke of B., who had kept her for a year. Then, for almost a further year she had entertained a succession of noble lovers, among them Lord J., who had kept her exclusively until a month ago, when she had gone to work in a very high-class house in Bayswater. There she found the great variety of lovers and the shallow attachments she formed with them much more to her taste than anything she had experienced before.

"But that," she said, offering me her slim little bottom, "was before tonight. You remember that thing you did to me first of all? Where you finished inside me? Would you like a long turn there, going all the way?"

"What is it called?" I asked.

"I have no idea. I have never permitted it to any man before tonight, no matter how they pleaded. But I did not know it could be so pleasant."

She gave out deep, guttural cries of pleasure all the way to our spending, which, again, was prodigious in the essence of joy if not in *essence de vie*.

We slept, I know not how long - perhaps only minutes, perhaps an hour. I awoke to find myself as fervent as ever to mount her - which I did, again from behind, but this time in nature's passage, riding her kneeling, lying, sideways, and with her on top - both of us staring at the ceiling. This last was the best, for it left my hands free to explore her cleft and caress her nipples, all of which racked her with new pleasures. Before that night I did not realize how exquisite a thing it is to assist a woman into an appreciation of her charms as great as my own - which, or so I take it, is where her pleasure chiefly resides. In other words, when a woman examines herself in the looking glass and is not displeased with what she sees, she is taking the first of a thousand steps, which end in that boundless whirlpool of sensation and ecstasy: the female climax. It is a phenomenon before which I am repeatedly humbled, for, no matter how often I may hear those whinnies and cries which are its outward sign, I am still amazed at its duration, at its possession of every nerve and vessel within her, at its profound grip on her very soul. I feel myself, as it were, an ape, struggling to comprehend the majesty of some grand human symphony.

Eventually, when she had jolted and writhed her frame to exhaustion and sweated a lake and cried herself hoarse, I could no longer hold myself back. As I spent I told her she was surely a goddess, having assumed a human form. At that her pleasure became so intense she passed out entirely.

And there, too, is another way in which women are finer than us men. For by far the greater part of her pleasure lies in knowing she is desired for something that is uniquely her – not her anatomical uniqueness, mind, though that may be a small part of it (else why consult the mirror at all!) – but some subtle blend of her personality and passion that no other woman on earth may mimic. When she knows her lover has discovered that uniqueness of hers and that all his desires revolve around it rather than the nothingness between her thighs, then she becomes a veritable pyromaniac of sexual delight and no common restraint can set limits to the flow of her pleasure, in which both she and her lover may drown while they will.

I lost count of the number of our drownings that night. Every time I awoke it was to find myself already hot and hard for another dip in that tenderest of pools – even at ten the following morning, when the beams of the sun stabbed my eyes and burned me into wakefulness – even then I found the Lad hard and willing once more.

All that day, whether we were at the four-leg frolic or not, her body and mine became like twins in the giving and taking of pleasure. I do not mean siblings, of course, but twins in purpose and expectation. We performed our ablutions, hastened into our unworn night attire, put on our dressing gowns, and sent for our breakfast, during which I, being the first to finish, slipped beneath the table and played the game that my vision of my aunt's oyster had added to my fantasies.

"Now you must let me feed on you," she said, and brought me back to bed, where she licked and sucked and kissed the Lad until he spent again. One single pearl was all he could disgorge by now, which she lifted in a kind of wonder on the tip of her finger and rubbed into the bridge of her nose.

That evening as the light began to fade she murmured, "Here it is, not yet twenty-four hours since you entered this room and you have given me more rogering than I get in a week from all comers in Bayswater – and more pleasure than I'd find there in a year. This is truly a Magic Wand." And she grasped the Lad firmly and shook him in vexation. "Oh, will *nothing* make him stay down!"

"Certainly," I told her. "If you go."

"You mean no amount of exercise will quell him?"

"I don't know," I replied. "Surely your experience can answer that."

"Hah! This is something so far outside my experience I hardly know where to begin."

And so I learned that my happy knack of staying hard and taking as much pleasure as I like of a woman – or as much as she's willing to grant me – is not universal among my fellow men. A doctor whom I trust – and I trust few of that breed – has informed me that boys of fourteen to sixteen can cheerfully shoot the bishop half a dozen times a day, but that by the time they are twenty, the power has waned to a mere three; at twenty-five, ten a week is hard going; thereafter the chronicle is too miserable to contemplate.

Well, I am now twenty-*seven* and I can, thanks be to the Great God Pan, still manage six a night (and a few more in the day) without flagging. To be sure, I do not produce those copious floods of sperm that fellows boast of in the saucy magazines you can pick up in Wych Street – all written by impotent old roués, or so that same doctor friend assures me. A teaspoon would be a good measure of my first salvo between wind and water; a single hollow pearl would easily hold my last. I have never understood the erotic fascination of those Niagaras of semen; apart from all else, just think of the mess – and the discomfort when the sheets turn cold and clammy!

No – like all the best medicines, my sperm comes in teaspoon quantities – "to be taken *ad libidum!*"

Where was I? Ah yes – *aetat* seventeen. Well, I endured a further year at Eton and then, having discovered not the faintest vestige of an academic gift, naturally went up to Balliol and began the only profession for which I have had any training or natural endowment – that of an idle and extremely rich young man. I was reared to it from the hour of my birth. I can truthfully say that since I was eighteen, the number of nights on which I have not enjoyed a woman at least once can be numbered on the fingers of one hand. Indeed, they could be numbered on the fingers of one *finger!*

Yes – one single night without the pleasure of a woman. It ought to have been three but I lost the wager after the first night. Morally, I still hold I won it, for the dainty little filly those rotters sent in to tempt me would have made short work of any saint you'd care to pit against her. I content myself with the knowledge that the wager was more honoured in her breach than in my observance.

So there it is. Superficially one might say that mine is a life rich in precocious promise and mature performance. At profounder levels, however, I have often felt that my almost boundless sexual gifts lay upon my shoulders the mantle of duty. The capacity of a woman, once she is roused, is almost infinite. Unhappily for most of them, the men with whom they seek satisfaction and relief cannot serve them beyond the once or twice and must then rest a full day round before they can go again. Most women, therefore, never rise to that crest of passion from which Pisgah height the Map of Life itself becomes at last visible in its joyous entirety; they die never knowing what they have missed. But I, being as tireless as the most wanton female that ever breathed, can match them all, sigh for sigh and spend for spend. I have thus been blessed with an almost unique insight into the wonderland of their desires and cravings. To take them by the hand and lead them, step by tender step, into that paradise is assuredly my sacred mission in life?

Much as young Eve had planned and anticipated this business between us, there remained one wild, unpurchased corner of her spirit that had not yet given her consent. I felt her stiffen the moment I undid that first button.

She shivered and sighed. I could see the pulse racing in her neck as I seated her on the chaise longue and knelt down behind her. She swallowed hard. "May I . . ." she faltered.

"No," I murmured. "You must leave it all to me, now. Do you feel as you imagined you would? Is this as your books foretold it?"

"No." It was a mere whisper.

I envied her as one envies anyone their first ride in a motor car, their first Turkish bath . . . indeed, all truly superb *first* experiences of anything.

I ran my hands inside her loosened bodice. Even today some well brought up young girls wear nothing beneath their dresses – just as in our grandmothers' time. Eve's underclothes comprised a simple bust bodice, suspended by two light shoulder straps and tied at the back by a drawstring that ran around below her breasts.

"What is the difference," I asked, "between this and your reading?" I loosened the tie and inserted my fingers just inside the bodice, beneath her armpits. I rested my fingernails where the softness of her breasts began.

She sighed again and whispered, "The actual . . . feel of you. I did not know . . ."

"Did you ever do this to yourself?" I asked, running my nails toward her nipples. They were superbly formed, those breasts – large and soft yet firm as peaches.

"It's not the same," she said.

I ran my nails over her nipples to their tip. Already generously swollen, they hardened at my touch. I squeezed them slowly between finger and thumb – squeezed and relaxed, squeezed and relaxed. She gave out an astonished "Oh!" and a "Hah!" An eavesdropper might have imagined I had hit her. "Oh that is so . . . so . . ." For once no word occurred to her.

"You have the most beautiful breasts I have felt in a long time," I murmured. "May I remove the bodice of your dress? Are there any more hooks or buttons?"

There were two. She reached her fingers down and slipped them free for me. Once the sleeves were past her elbows, the whole of it fell away. I lifted the bust bodice and rested it gently on the tops of those adorable breasts; the swelling of her nipples looked almost painful to me as I rubbed them in big, gentle circles against my stretched palms. Then, increasing the pressure, I turned her and eased her down until she was half lying on the seat and backrest.

Smiling at me, a lazy, stupefied smile, she brought up both her legs, trying to fold them half under her – as eighteen years of training in modesty had taught her to do. I gently eased them apart and pushed them down again, until they were at rest on the floor, one each side of our couch. Her smile grew dreamier still.

"Nothing to say now?" I asked.

She shook her head and closed her eyes. That seraphic little smile intrigued me. She was not the sort of girl to yield so utterly and so soon. Was she thinking of Wilhelmina, asleep next door – her possible competitor for this very position? I still sensed that inner core of reserve somewhere there inside her, the bastion and citadel of her will not to yield. I have known girls who can give you every inch of their bodies while they retire to that inner keep and watch you as you loot and pillage the rest, searching for that elusive *je ne sais quoi*. Ladies of easy virtue do it all the time, to be sure; but one knows that's their game; and *they* know it, too. The trick is to surprise or entice them out of it – which I am invariably able to do, if not the first time, then the second or third or fourth. But inexperienced young girls like Eve aren't even supposed to realize what's happening. It was a delicious challenge, of course, and I turned to her with redoubled purpose.

The sight of a young girl, a virgin, lying back half-clothed in such a lascivious position, smiling and utterly relaxed, is vastly stimulating – better than a stupendous win at cards even. I became more determined than ever to make her realize how fortunate she was to have chosen me as her tutor in these arts.

Slowly, wanting to rush nothing, I raised the hem of her skirt. She had underneath a couple of cotton petticoats, one plain, one with a single frill - very young-girlish. Her stockings, too, were of unembroidered cotton. No garters. Utterly delightful after all the frenchified goods I'd waded through recently.

My hands went exploring on up - sufficiently far to discover that her trim little waist owed nothing to corsets; her only nether garment, beneath her skirt and petticoats, was a pair of plain cotton drawers of the old-fashioned kind with an open crotch. No corset? I felt again, for I could not believe it. Her waist was trim, like a child's, yet her hips were as ample as a fully grown woman's. I cannot remember another girl whose body swells so naturally and with such delicate grace from a waist so slim to a pair of hips so generous. It set me trembling anew.

When she felt the first draft of night air on her Temple of Hymen, she gave out a shivery little sigh and slid herself even further toward me. I lowered my lips to her thighs, just above and inside her knees, where her stockings ended. And there I began a slow, tender caress, exploring her with long, sweeping movements - upward, relentlessly upward, toward that ultimate goal whose delicate pink folds I could so plainly see. The nearer I got, the wider she spread herself for me, finally revealing the sweetest young fig I had seen in many a year. Its outer lips were swollen and feverish; the inner ones an almost burning red, but finely curved and beautifully formed, like the keels of two canoes; they parted to give me a glimpse of a tight little bullseye, still veiled in that membrane whose life was now measured in minutes. The pale, hard bunch of her rosebud was most endearing of all, like a tiny emblem of manhood welded to her skin. I put my tongue to it and started to work.

I had been with too many whores of late, who bathe themselves a score of times a day when there is nothing to launder but their own shame; all taste and fragrance of Woman has long gone out of them. I had forgotten the full magic of it until I put my tongue to my young Eve's flower and filled my senses with her nectar.

She had read of this activity but nothing had prepared her for the majestic touch and feel of it. I envy women that sensation. With us it is thrilling enough when a skilled woman takes us between her lips and works away with an experienced tongue. But the exquisite joy of it is not *inside* us, as it is with women. We merely *feel* our thrill; they truly *possess* it.

And I envied Eve especially, feeling for the first time in her life a living tongue down there - and a tongue that had tasted a thousand others and now carried all their pleasures in its competence. It is whatever you ask of it, my tongue - a feather, a tender claw, a volcano, a fumarole, an eel, a silver dart, an entire hand. I could have relished that darling oyster of hers all night. But I recalled I had a higher purpose in this, beyond my own selfish pleasure.

There are two ways to handle a virgin and leave her eager for more. If she is passionate by nature and easily roused, it is best to build her climax in time with your own, so that you arrive in those magical uplands of Eros together. But if she is slow or reluctant - if part of her stays in that shell of self-denial - then by all means lift her to that plateau first, and help her explore its amazements while you are still on your climb.

Thus, as I feasted for my pleasure, I increased hers,

awaiting that moment when I could catch her unawares. Far away, miles above my head, I heard her breathing grow even more wildly disordered, now catching itself in deep-drawn sighs and gasps of astonishment, now panting as her delight continued to swell. And yet that hard nugget of reserve was in her still. Most men would not have noticed it; for that I must thank my almost supernatural ability to please the gentle sex – which would be impossible without my almost mystical understanding of their most secret ravishments. I could feel it there, that persistent reserve of hers, like a third party, watching all I did. And, yet, such was my skill, her sweet surrender into the whirlpool of misrule drew inexorably on. Judging my moment, I reached for her breasts and began again to caress her nipples, folding them gently up and down. My fingers ambushed that wildness in her, that resistant core, overwhelming it with sensations too sudden and too astoundingly sweet to bear.

She uttered one long, astonished whimper of surrender and reached her pelvis at me, grabbing for more of this new elixir that seemed to flow from my tongue into every nerve and vein of her suddenly electrified body. I gave her all she could have desired, producing a second and then a third detonation of her craving flesh. Then, unbuttoning myself and giving the Lad some air, I made the swiftest substitute of him for my tongue.

Dreamily she opened her eyes and looked at him – my old, scarlet-faced, one-eyed ruffian who never sleeps until I am sated. "Oh!" she sighed, putting her hand over his head and pressing him firmly to her. "Now! Now!"

I kept the impatient fellow caressing and browsing there among her folds and stubble until I felt her rising once again. Bit by bit I eased back his pressure against her, making her reach for the touch of him, lifting herself up and up, grabbing for him with an ever-widening crevice and stretching her maidenhead ever more taut for the sacrificial kill. When she was at her limit I pulled back and went into her in one clean thrust, only an inch or so but enough to make the break. She would have collapsed, gasping and sobbing in a mingled torrent of pleasure and relief, but I had my hands firmly under her *derrière* and kept her up there.

A beautiful, dainty ring of scarlet wept out of her and garlanded my lance of love. There was no pain in her moaning, no grimace of discomfort on her face, so I began to let him go gently in and out, a fraction deeper each time, relishing the feel of her dumb glutton parting ahead of me – also the knowledge that mine was the first bowsprit ever to dock in that warm, juicy haven, so tight and so smooth. When there was still an inch or so of me to go, I felt the Lad's crown nudge against her gullet. Her face puckered with the discomfort. Then I withdrew a little and, lying full stretch upon her, began to poke away with an absolutely regular rhythm, withdrawing the Lad to her outermost lips each stroke but never touching her gullet again on the opposite thrust.

My profound experience of women warned me it would have been a mistake to introduce a virgin to every room in the Halls of Pleasure, all at once. Her First Night, when it is the first of many, is but the anteroom to a whole palace of erotic bliss. Even in that anteroom, though, I could feel that my darling young Eve was lost to me, lost to the world . . . lost in some interior exploration of sensations she had never dreamed were there to discover. I chose that even rhythm, matching it to her breathing, to those small, involuntary movements all girls make in their ecstasy, to give her, as it were, the groundswell, over which she could herself navigate the frail *Golden Hind* of sexual discovery. Wave upon wave upon wave I freely gave that craft.

Soon she was held by my very regularity; knowing it was there, knowing I should not let her down, she could safely launch herself into her own pools of sensual delight, there to seek that sweetest oblivion of all - soaring on waves of one long and infinitely available orgasm. Her cries and gasps of delight and the little whimpers and moans she made in between were balm to me. I was not so fond as to imagine I had vanquished her reserve for ever; indeed, I expected *her*, that untouchable Eve, to return at dawn with triple-proof armour and twice as vigilant. But I had shown the *other* her, the real Eve, what an alliance with me would yield in dividends of joy.

Her cries grew increasingly desperate; the shudders that racked her body were now so deep and violent I thought she might pass out. I was then but a single squeeze away from my own climax. "Now!" I cried, raising myself and throwing my thighs outside hers to scoop them together and make her oracle pinch my Lad as hard as possible. She felt every squirt of my coming like a new explosion inside her. She stared up at me, eyes like saucers, jaw wide open, and then exploded in one final climax of her own, the mightiest of all.

I could have gone again at once - and, indeed, was almost tempted to show off to her that way. But my profound sexual wisdom, which sometimes amazes even me, told me that her body was now so crammed with new sensations to digest, new responses to recall and re-explore, that it would be best to call this the night and look for more tomorrow.

I carried her to our bed and waited for her to fall

asleep. I could not remember the last time I had enjoyed but a single dip with a young girl – especially such a warm little beauty as Eve. Most of my pleasure – apart from the occasional servant girl and the wives of careless friends – has been with cyprians. With them I always bargain for "two hours and as many spendings as I can." They smile knowingly, thinking they've heard that one before and I'll droop at two. Well, they soon learn! If they're not bathed in the sweat of ecstasy and begging me to stop before half our time is up – and then begging me to continue, the moment I obey – I go straight from them to Harley Street in a cab and a high old panic.

So to desist at the first shot between wind and water was a true mark of my refinement and sensibility. It also put me in mind of dear young Wilhelmina, fast asleep next door.

When Eve was breathing regularly – and giving out little sighs as, no doubt, she rehearsed our frolics in some restrospective dream – I eased away from her and slipped out of bed. I undressed fully before I walked around to dowse the lamp. I hadn't gone two paces before I realized we were not alone. For there, in the doorway to the dressing room, her naked body barely a glimmer against the dimness beyond, stood Miss Wilhelmina Clark. She vanished at once and I heard the dressing-room bed creak.

I took the lamp and went after her. She lay with her dark, curly tresses spilled in disorder on the pillow, pretending to be as fast asleep as I had supposed her to be all this while. I placed the lantern on her bedside table. Suddenly I realized I was standing, rather thoughtlessly, with the Lad proud as a peacock and only an inch or so from her face. It was a vision of Pure Beauty that set me all a-tremble. I dropped to my knees and continued to stare at her. It *was* a plain face; again I could not deny it. And yet it possessed a simple, wholesome goodness that mere prettiness would have spoiled. Little though I knew of her, I already felt much warmer toward her than ever I had to the sleeping Miss Bassington, even at the height of our pleasure together.

Without opening her eyes she smiled and murmured, ‘You were right in one thing, my lord: If you prick me, I shall bleed.’’

I chuckled and, placing my lips close to her ear, whispered, ‘‘My dear, dark angel of the night – I cannot possibly take such an assertion on trust.’’

She opened her eyes then and her whole face was transformed. The dim lamplight reflected in those two dark pools of passion and mystery and I was pierced to the very core.

She raised her sheets a millionth of an inch; it was enough. Oh, the furnace heat of that ample, soft young body! I began to caress her in a fever of rekindled desire, but she murmured, ‘‘Don’t wait,’’ and I knew she had been watching Eve and me, perhaps from the very beginning.

The Lad was already wandering half-lost in those wet, slippery folds between her thighs. Which of them were the agreeable ruts of life and which the actual centre of bliss I could not tell until I felt the momentary resistance of her maidenhead, which parted around my lancet like a fine scissors of skin. She gave an ambiguous little cry, which could have been pain or pleasure, and then clutched at my buttocks and pulled so hard I gasped at her strength.

There was no plumbing the depth of that fleshy burrow, not with my modest eight inches. It was soft and sinuous, lavish in its folds and wrinkles. She had muscles there whose existence, I’m sure, she had not until then suspected. She discovered them now, though – and took me so much by surprise I came at once – while she was still down there in the foothills. As I returned toward the fringe of my delirium I could feel the disappointment sinking through her like a pail of lead. But how I relished her delight when I turned her over and started once again, hard and big as before, this time from her rear.

Twice more I gave her that thrill and surprise before she cried off and begged for respite. As I lay at her side, replete at last, she asked me, "Do *you* think I'm fat and ugly?"

"There is a beauty in you," I assured her, "whose secret Cleopatra herself would have thought cheap for half the wealth of Egypt."

"Are you going to pick me, then? Or that cool, pretty creature snoring next door?"

I tickled her under the chin and said, "Tell me what it was like and I'll give you my reply."

I could feel her running through all the conventional answers; then she said, "You know those absurd plays they love to bring round to village halls – where mothers and sons who haven't met for twenty years recognize each other at once – by some magical sympathy? Well, it was like that. I recognized it just like that – just as absurd and just as magical." When she felt I did not grasp her point, she added, "You have united parts of me that might otherwise have lived out my life in total ignorance of each other's existence. I don't know if you wanted to hear something as selfish as that, but it's the truth. I'm sure you don't need me to tell you what a wonderful lover you are. Now – what's your answer?"

"Tomorrow morning early," I whispered, "someone will bring Eve and me a cup of tea. Come and join us then. Dress, optional."

'That's not fair – you said you'd tell me."

"So I did. And now I've told you when."

'What d'you call 'early'?"

"About seven."

She rolled away from me, moaned, "Oh my God," and appeared to fall asleep.

The following morning at ten past seven, my man Nimrod brought our tea and Marie biscuits; three cups on the tray; capital fellow. I asked him to be so good as to go to the dressing room and invite Miss Clark to join us. That woke up Eve with a bump! "That fat baggage?" she cried. I caressed various parts of her delectable body, which remembered that touch and conspired to silence her tongue, if only temporarily.

Wilhelmina came yawning into the room, immediately behind Nimrod. She was wearing one of my nightshirts, which covered her amplitude from neck to ankle. Eve stared daggers at her as she climbed in on the far side of me; she smiled ever so sweetly back. "You may pour our tea and leave, Nimrod," I told him. "Return with my shaving water in about five minutes."

"I have news, my lord," he replied.

"Good or bad?"

"That would be for you to determine, my lord."

"Oh God, that's too much to ask of a fellow at seven in the morning. Tell me when I've breakfasted."

"As you wish, my lord." Ominously he added, "It's not the sort of news that simply goes away on its own."

The moment he closed the door behind him Eve snapped, "You could have asked him to get *me* one of your beastly nightshirts, too. I'm not sitting up naked with her all dressed."

Wilhelmina rose at once, folding down the sheets to

reveal she had meanwhile removed that garment. She breathed deeply and raised her arms while she combed her fingers through her hair. Eve sat up and did other things to display her equally fetching allurements.

"If all these spellbinding eurythmics could be devoted to producing one cup of tea, unspilled, in each of our laps, I should think myself in paradise," I commented.

Eve hastened to oblige, not least because it gave her the chance to show off her trim waist, her supple back, and her delicious *derrière* – and just a glimpse of the dark folds of her crevice, toward the back. She took her time, in case I missed the first five minutes. We sipped and munched in a ruminative silence, neither girl wishing to be the first to reveal she was in any way eager to learn which had won the competition between them; and I wondering how to tell them what I had, in fact, decided. Also I was relishing my biscuit, and the warm feeling I always get when two naked young girls are at my side, and the future of bliss which, I now felt sure, stretched before me.

There followed a truce during which I shaved and we each saw to our various ablutions. Then, refreshed and reinvigorated, we returned to our couch of bliss. They each lay at my side and threw an arm about me, moving it this way and that until neither girl touched the other at any point.

"The first thing to assure you both," I said, "is that bank accounts will be opened in your name this morning and a generous deposit made into each. The sum was mentioned in my letter to your parents, I believe . . ."

"I will accept no more than one hundred," Wilhelmina said quickly. "I cannot believe I am worth even that much – *yet.*"

"I could not take a penny," Eve riposted swiftly.

"For me it was a *pure* night of pleasure."

"You'll take exactly what you're given," I told them. "Because it is the sugar that coats what I fear will be a bitter pill to both of you."

They stopped breathing for a moment.

"You see," I said mournfully, "I simply did not think far enough ahead. The entire affair – as I've already explained to Miss Bassington – resulted from a bet . . ."

This time I went on to explain its nature.

"How many did you find?" Wilhelmina asked. "Gentlemen who would be willing to sell their daughters, I mean?"

"Several hundred."

They digested this news in glum silence. "My God!" Eve exclaimed at last. "How can people be such hypocrites!"

"The point is," I went on, "I never had any intention of choosing any girl, or of . . ."

"You mean . . . no Paris, no Vienna . . . none of that?" Wilhelmina was aghast.

Eve smiled sweetly at me, to remind me how little such externals had mattered to her. The other saw it – and understood it – all in a flash. With the most insouciant of laughs she said, "Such a disappointment would have mortified me . . . before last night!"

"Listen girls," I interrupted, "this entire discussion is pointless. You see – until last night I have sought my pleasure among . . . women of a certain class. You understand what I mean, I hope?"

'Harlots," Eve said.

"Ah . . . precisely. And there, you see, the arrangement is quite straightforward. I buy two hours of their time and use their bodies as I desire – which usually means at least half a dozen such encounters as we enjoyed last night."

"And then each week you find another?" Wilhelmina guessed, supposing me to mean that my six spendings were spread over as many days.

"Well, no," I admitted reluctantly. "I usually wait until the following night. Half a dozen good sessions in an evening usually leave me pretty satisfied for the rest of the night."

After a pause Eve swallowed heavily. "*Half a dozen,* you say?"

I cleared my throat, signalling a small concession. "Encounters with such females are not terribly satisfactory, you know. I find I must make up in quantity what they lack in quality. Until you reminded me last night – both of you – I had forgotten what depths of true pleasure it is possible to reach with young girls who have no need to counterfeit their joys."

"Is *that* what they do?" Wilhelmina asked. "D'you know, it's the one thing that's always puzzled me about them."

"So you believe you might manage with fewer?" Eve persisted. "Er . . . two, perhaps?"

"Or three?" Wilhelmina put in her bid.

"Yes, or three?" Eve countered hastily.

I sighed. "Possibly . . ." My tone made it sound the wishfullest of thinking. "But I'd hate to feel constrained in that way – you know? To use up my dole of three and then lie there sweating with frustration while you – *one* of you – slept on at my side." I lay back fully and spread my thighs wide. "Especially," I added, "when I find I adore each of you equally."

"Then take me," Wilhelmina cried, throwing herself upon me with her thighs parted over my left, squirming to give herself a little ecstasy upon it.

“No, me!” Eve cried. “I got to him first.” She threw herself on my other thigh and, being slimmer, squirmed twice as furiously.

“But you obviously failed to satisfy him,” Wilhelmina said, going breathless at my left ear.

“Stop!” I cried, laying my hands on their wriggling bottoms and pressing them to a halt. Would they never grasp my purpose? “When I say I adore you both equally, it is not that you are equal at all – except in the sense that you are the equal and perfect complement of each other . . .”

“Meaning I’m pretty and she’s . . . not?” Eve cut in.

“Meaning you are exquisitely pretty, my pet, which an ape with half an eye could see in the dark – while she has a beauty that requires a rare judgement to appreciate – the sort of judgement you must pray you will one day acquire. What I mean is I could not choose one of you without mourning for ever the relinquishment of the other.”

Now, for the love of the Great God Pan, surely . . .?

After a longish silence Wilhelmina murmured, “There is one possible way out . . .”

I nodded. “I can hardly be the one to suggest it to two delicate and refined young ladies.”

They raised their heads above me, glanced at each other, and then, putting their lips to my ears, whispered, “Have both of us.”

For the best part of the next hour that is what I did, right royally – passing from one to the other in the most delightful innocence; I mean they did not touch each other. And when they finally begged mercy I showed them how to use the douche while I lay back once more and watched them – and contemplated yet again all the happy weeks or months that lay ahead.

And that was when Nimrod came in and told me he

had "put the other two young females in the other house, just round the corner."

I sat up at that, and so, metaphorically, did the two girls. They stared accusingly at me. I stared in slight bewilderment at Nimrod. "What other two?" I asked. "And come to that, what other house?"

"A Miss G–H– and a Miss Angela Parkin, sir. Parkin is Miss G–'s maid and will come in at half price, she says."

"Who says?"

"Miss G–, my lord."[*In the manuscript these names were originally written in full and later excised. I explain why in my postscript to this volume. FR*]

"What other house?" Eve echoed.

"The house you won off of Colonel Trotter, my lord, when you were taking bets on . . ."

"Yes, yes! Never mind what we were betting about. It is very tedious of you to remember it in such circumstances as this. But to my own certain recollection, *that* house is in Aberdeen – which can hardly be described as 'just around the corner,' eh?"

"Pardon my appearing to contradict you, my lord, but the house is, in fact, in Aberdeen *Gardens* – which is not a furlong from here."

I stared at him in utter amazement. "Good heavens! D'you mean to say . . . but see here, what am I doing with this villa then?"

"You rented it, my lord."

"Of course I know that, you oaf! The question is why? Why did I rent this villa when I already had a perfectly good place around the corner? It *is* a perfectly good place, is it not?"

"I did wonder at the time, my lord. And yes, it is a perfectly good place – much larger than this and better" – he cleared his throat in a significant way – *"appointed."*

Eve tapped my knees. "If the thwarted house agent inside you is now satisfied, my darling, and if there's one tiny little particle of you that's at all interested in Miss G– and her cut-price maid, I'm sure both Miss Clark and I would be obliged if you'd give *his* curiosity a little airing."

I raised a laconic eyebrow at my man. He pursed his lips and gave a confidential nod at all three of us. "Most delectable," he said. "Most."

We decided to take breakfast at once and, pausing only to dismiss the servants, walk around the corner to Aberdeen Gardens and see . . . well, whatever we should see.

The morning was well advanced, however, before we left my villa; and by then my mood was very far from what may be imagined.

I should never have left my two young mistresses to their own toilette. Women – and though I adore them more than any man alive, I have to allow this – women are born deceivers. And not so much of men as of each other.

Now I have no doubt in my own mind but that those two adorable things had enjoyed with me the greatest ecstasy of which their young, untutored, inexperienced bodies were capable. Yet the moment they found themselves alone together, and imagining me to be in the servants' hall dismissing the whole wretched pack without a character (which, indeed, I did – and it required all of two minutes) – the moment they were alone together, I say, they began encouraging each other into that species of foul blackguardism of which only the finest and noblest women are capable.

"He is indeed a superb lover," Wilhelmina was

saying as I returned to my dressing room – they being in my bedroom, just beyond the open door.

Naturally my best instincts rebelled at playing the eavesdropper, and yet I felt I deserved no lesser reward for all my skill at showing them what wonderlands lay between their thighs.

"I've read so much about it," Eve replied, "and even so I never imagined it might be like that."

"Mind you," Wilhelmina countered, "I must confess he has left me a little sore."

"Me too," Eve agreed. "In fact, more than a little. Quite a lot. He went at me very hard."

"And yet he is a wonderful lover."

"Oh yes! Wonderful, wonderful." After a silence Eve added, "Even so, there were moments – just one or two – when I could have wished him gentler and more considerate of my feelings."

"I know what you mean." Pause. "Nonetheless, there is an undeniable excitement in his impetuosity, don't you find? It is like a rushing mountain torrent that sweeps all before it."

"Now and then," Eve said judiciously. "Yes, I was swept up now and then, I grant him that. But there were also times when I simply lay there, beached and grounded beneath that cascade of his desire . . . and wondering . . . well, no, that would be unkind."

"What? You were wondering what?"

"No, no, forget I mentioned it. One should not be so carping and censorious. After all, I'm sure he *meant* well."

Wilhelmina sighed. "And he did derive such pleasure from it himself. We must comfort our spirits with that reflection. To give so much pleasure to a man is itself a *kind* of pleasure, too . . . don't you think?"

"Y-e-s." Eve drew out the word, as if her agreement

were more polite than heartfelt. "I found the way to make him finish quickly is to thrash around and sigh and moan and gasp as if one were in the last throes of delight oneself. Perhaps you overheard me?"

"No! No!" Wilhelmina hastened to assure her.

Of course, I now realized what was going on between them. They were ashamed of their own abandon and were seeking to put the best possible face on it – parading their indifference like a badge of female honour; but my understanding did nothing to diminish my fury that they could so abuse something which had surely been sacred to us all only a few short hours ago. *There* you have the perfidy of woman at its starkest!

"I'm so relieved to hear you confess how sore he made you," Wilhelmina went on. "I truly did not know how I could face the same onslaught again tonight – and tomorrow, and tomorrow, and all our tomorrows. Do you think we might induce him to take on these other two girls as well? It would relieve us of half the burden of his attentions, don't you see?" After a silence she added, "And I'm sure it would not affect his generosity. He seems to have more oof than anyone could possibly need."

Eve pulled a face. Though I couldn't see her, I heard it in her voice. "But one of them is a maidservant! How can we share him with a servant?"

Wilhelmina cleared her throat delicately. "We are already sharing him with the commonest drabs from the gutters, my dear."

"True. True." Eve sighed.

There was a long silence while they attended to their features.

"What were you going to say just now?" Wilhelmina prompted.

"When?"

"You said you just lay there under the torrent of his passion and found yourself wondering . . . what?"

"Oh?" Eve laughed as if she had genuinely forgotten. "I just wondered, 'Is that *it?*' Is that what we've been warned against all our lives? Is that the unbelievable, unimaginable, overpowering, *thing* to guard against which we've been kept in virtual imprisonment all these years? *That?* I simply couldn't believe it."

"Oh, how alike we are beneath the skin!" Wilhelmina cried.

I turned and left them to their treason.

And yet . . . and yet . . . I found myself thinking.

Was I being a little harsh? They were, indeed, two refined and well-brought-up young ladies – virgins of impeccable Middle Class origins. My superb skills as a lover had tricked them into a passion they had been reared to think of as ugly and sinful. Each was now consumed with the fear that the other had heard her whinnying like a mare at stand; their first thoughts in the blear light of day must be to explain and condone that seeming abandonment of all their former morality.

How dull I was not to have seen it! Perhaps, I began to think, I am not quite the erotic maestro I fancy myself as being? My experience of women up until that moment may have been profound, yet it was hardly broad. Had my sensibilities been coarsened by my confining myself to one class of amorous partner – and a very Lower Class at that?

The moment I started on this tack there was no return to my former serenity of mind. I began to castigate myself more harshly than either of my two little dears had done – and with greater justice and accuracy, too. I realized I had behaved last night, to all intents and purposes, just like the chaps in the Wych Street magazines – *The Pearl,* and so on – you know them: Fellow meets girl; fellow handles girl; girl says, "Unhandle me, sir. Fie! etc."; fellow pays not a blind bit of notice; girl drops her objections and, in short order, her drawers as well; they go at it like rabbits, eight times in a row . . . she's a virgin, blood all over the place . . . "Oh God how you hurt me but please don't stop!" . . . torrents of semen . . .

The only reason for stopping is that the poor old writer has run out of ink. He ran out of semen (his own, you follow) years ago. Next night, identical frolics except the girl has a different name . . . and so on, *passim,* for a hundred pages.

Of course, in my case it wasn't quite so bad as that. My impeccable breeding and refinement spared me and my two sweet loves from the worst of that absurdity. And yet, in essence, that had been the way of it last night.

What could I have been thinking of? How could I have overlooked the possibilities – nay, the challenge – now presented to me by sweet young Eve and my dear little Wilhelmina? Two pretty young virgins of such impeccable upbringing who had volunteered themselves to me for a season of amorous service. And that was all I had seen in them: two temporary mistresses to swell the ranks of my cyprian partners!

Treacherous though their conversation was – and hurtful as it might have been to one who understood the female soul less well than I – it restored me to my proper sensibilities. I now realized that when a girl from such a background crosses that particular Rubicon, she burns every boat and bridge behind her. She can never return to the dull round of county balls and subscription concerts and all those tedious ceremonies whereby the Middle Classes cement their piffling little alliances. The girl who cannot carry the jewel of her maidenhead into those rituals cannot carry a husband out of them, either.

So last night, the moment I deprived them of that fair diadem, I, as a man of honour, assumed responsibility for their two futures. These were no Covent Garden flowers who could be abandoned to fend for themselves in the common hedgerow. So, the question now arose: If not the regular bourgeois marriage, then what?

They could not remain my mistresses forever – for that in itself would turn into a kind of uncertificated wedlock. I could see no other thing for it but that they must marry into the aristocracy, where these things matter much less. I could name half a dozen lords who had married girls no better than they ought to be. Lord Melton, for instance. Only last year he married Peg Jarvis, whom *I* had found the year before, drunk and sobbing outside Kate Hamilton's House in Piccadilly. It was I who made a lady of her, as even Melton himself had the grace to admit when he made her a Lady.

And what about the old Earl of Strathclyde, eh? Married Sally Giddings, my first mistress after I got sent down from Oxford . . .

The hair rose on my neck as the import of these random memories was born in upon me. I am not a ruminative sort of chap. The last thing in the world you're ever likely to catch me at is sitting down having a good long think about my life and Where It's All Going To End Up. But I'm not so blind that I can't see a pattern when it steps up and bites me like that.

My way ahead was now plain: If I couldn't have the time of my life with these two most adorable young girls – and afterwards marry them off into the aristocracy – then, by the Great God Pan, I deserved their treacherous contumely!

As we walked out into the sunlight of a bright February morn, Wilhelmina gave a frisky little skip and took my arm. "Oh," she said, "I think I must truly be the happiest girl alive."

Eve, not to be outdone, took my other arm and said, "Bar one."

They giggled. I sighed. The grave responsibilities I had undertaken with the sentimental education of my two young acolytes were just beginning to bear in upon me.

"Oh come," Eve responded. "Why so heavy? What do we call you, by the way – my lord? Lord H?"

"Hardy, will do."

"Is that your name?"

"No, but it's sort of stuck to me since school."

"Well, Hardy," Eve repeated, "why these heavy sighs?"

"I'm wondering what would be the kindest thing to say to turn off these two young hopefuls."

"You haven't even seen them yet," Wilhelmina said sharply.

"No, but I know already that, were they each Helen of Troy and Cleopatra and Venus herself, all rolled into one, I should still not feel the slightest desire for them. You, my fair young nymphs, are all I want. Oh, I cannot tell you what a profound and moving pleasure it is to me to know that ahead of us stretch limitless days and nights of such frolicking as we have now embarked on!"

I paused to let them assure me they wanted nothing better – which, eventually, they did.

"And believe me, my darlings, the little hors

d'oeuvres we tasted last night and this morning were as nothing to the carousing on which we shall now gorge and satiate our flesh."

They said nothing. I asked were they not overjoyed to hear it. Wanly, they agreed that they were.

"And yet . . ." said Eve.

"Yes," echoed Wilhelmina. "And yet . . ."

"What?" I prompted.

"Well," Eve continued carefully, "when Nimrod mentioned these other two – G– and Abigail, is it? – at the very mention of their names . . . oh, you will think me most the most forward and abandoned creature for saying this, but I felt a *frisson* – yes, a decided *frisson* – of amatory delight at the thought that four of us might frolic together in the one bed, and with such a divine lover to still our unbridled desires."

"Oh!" Wilhelmina exclaimed.

Eve raised a hand. "Call me wanton if you will, yet I swear . . ."

"No, no!" cried her sister in duplicity . . . why do I call her that? Do I convey any information thereby – other than that they were two women with but one purpose? No matter. She cried, "No, no!" and then added: " 'Twas admiration, dear sister, caused me so to exclaim. For now let me confess I felt it equally, but was too ashamed of my dissolute spirit to admit it. I felt my knees tremble and my innards turn all hollow at the thought." She squeezed my arm. "Come up now, Hardy! You are surely no prude in this. Confess it – your desires quicken, too, at the prospect of a four-in-hand where now you may ride but a pair of young fillies?"

My silence provoked them to provoke me, to lean forward, to peer at me, to smile, giggle, laugh, dig me in the ribs . . .

Reluctantly, I smiled, too. "Now by the Great God Pan," I declared, "how have I deserved two such devoted and selfless votaries as you? You shame me with your singleminded dedication to that goddess who now rules all our lives. By heavens, G– and Abigail *shall* remain with us and share our ceremonies, inspiring me to fourfold efforts to please you all."

Their joy at this promise was not quite so unconfined as their earlier protestations might have led me to expect. But I pressed on, for we were almost at the house by now. "See here," I said, "these arrangements between us have come about in so higgledy-piggledy a manner – and were, in any case, based on an advertisement and a letter that were never seriously intended . . . and now there are to be four of you . . . well, well, in short, I think we must place ourselves on . . . I shall not say a more formal footing, but at least on one that is better thought out than this."

"Yes?" they asked with wary politeness. "In what way?"

"You see," I explained gently, "we are none of us destined to remain together for life. This is no contract of marriage between us. Now, if I took no thought beyond my own selfish pleasure, I should say what happens after is your own affair and no concern of mine. But I find I cannot be so cavalier with such sweet and adorable creatures as you have proved – and will no doubt prove with doubled and redoubled vitality in the weeks ahead, as your addiction to my ardent parts grows as slavish as mine already is to yours. So – with your consent – we shall set ourselves the ambition of turning you into such adepts in the arts of love that, when we part in joyful remembrance, you will all marry above the rank of baronet."

If I had stuffed grenades down their bodices I could

not have jolted them more. And that, in turn, set my rusty old brain cogs whirring. My conclusions were so blindingly obvious I could only confess myself a fool for not having reached them the moment I saw Miss Bassington at the Albany last night.

My life of easy lechery - coupled with my reading of the classics of erotic fiction - had led me into the error of supposing that women's desires are no different from men's and that we all spend fifty-nine minutes of every waking hour wondering how our next tumble together is to be contrived. Unthinkingly I had assumed that the thoughts uppermost in my mind also swayed the minds of these two young doves and had caused them to fly the parental nest.

Yet how could that be? What did they know of me? My picture is never in the papers. I avoid all society occasions - even those from which my reputation has not already barred me. For all that young Eve and Wilhelmina knew, I might have been toothless, bald, and sixty. They were not fleeing *to* Lord Hornington. They were not fleeing *to* anything - least of all to a life of erotic delight. They were fleeing *from* their dreary families, their dismal prospects, their unspeakable Middle Class lives, cribb'd, cabbin'd and confined. If they had entertained even the vaguest thought of opening their thighs, it was as no more than a kind of forfeit or penalty they must pay to escape Something Worse at home.

"You mean a kind of school?" Wilhelmina asked, being the first to recover.

"Marry above a baronet?" echoed Eve. "Now how you can be sure of securing us that?"

I slipped my arm about her - we were entering the driveway by now - and gave a gentle squeeze. "I may be lamentably ignorant," I confessed, "of the feelings that swell a young girl's bosom, but of the matrimonial proclivites of the nobility, permit me to be your infallible guide."

"But I thought you all married each other and were terribly inbred."

"You shall see," was all I had time to say. Then, turning to answer Wilhelmina's question, I said, "Let us rather call it an academy. Yes!" I was in love with the notion already, though it was less than a minute old. "Lord Hornington's Academy of Love!"

A grinning Nimrod was waiting at the door. From the outside the house was like any other in that outer suburb of London; but the opulence of the interior took my breath away – especially when I remembered old Trotter, who had struck me as rather austere, exactly the kind of fellow you'd expect to own a house in Aberdeen. The impression was of an oriental harem, with marble pillars and arcades everywhere, draped with fans and feathers and silks, and an all-pervading whiff of incense. Nimrod beckoned us forward to a screen of pierced stone that lined all one length of the entrance hall; through it we saw our two visitors waiting for us in a conventionally furnished morning room. There was no mistaking which of them was which.

Miss G–H– was about nineteen years old. She had auburn hair and large greeny-grey eyes. Her milk-white skin was stretched taut over her bones and covered in fine freckles. Her bosom was small but pleasingly shaped; her ankle, neat. The remainder was, for the moment, a matter of blissful conjecture. Beautiful in a remote sort of way, she was standing with her back to the empty fireplace, holding a sketchbook in her hand, and drawing her maid, Abigail Parkin.

Miss Parkin was a tall, slender seventeen-year-old

with deep red hair. She, too, was freckled, but hers were few and large. Her bosom was as small as that of her mistress, but she was as yet tender in years. Hers was an interesting face, neither pretty nor plain, but full of character.

"Miss H–," I called out cheerily as we entered the room. "Allow me to present two young friends of mine, Miss Eve Bassington, who comes from the Wirral, and Miss Wilhelmina Clark, who is from Gloucester." Miss G– told us she was the daughter of a wholesale merchant in Edinburgh.

While they were busy shaking hands I turned to the maid. "And you, I presume, are Miss Abigail Parkin?" I shook her hand warmly, much to her astonishment. Three lots of hackles rose behind me. "I'm so glad you came, Miss Parkin. Tell me, is it your intention to stay? Or will you return to Scotland now you have delivered your mistress safely to me?"

She was nervous, gazelle-like, swift in her movements even when they were slight; I felt she might dart away and hide at the slightest provocation. I wanted her more than all the rest; there was something haunting, elusive about her that I had to explore.

Miss G– answered for her. "It was the only condition on which I was allowed to escape," she said bitterly. "Don't let those big, shy eyes deceive you, Lord Hornington. She's tough as nails, that one."

Miss Parkin lowered her eyes and smiled as if she had just been paid the greatest compliment. I looked back at Miss G– and realized that her bluntness had not replaced her earlier, rather remote demeanour, but simply joined it. It struck me she might be as mercurial as the wind. Perhaps that was why Miss Parkin took it so mildly.

I explained to them the muddle over the location and ownership of this house and asked if they would mind accompanying me while I went on a swift tour of inspection. Of course, being women, they were even more eager than I – if that were possible. A whore once told me that what finally persuaded her to the work was the unbelievable luxury of the bed she had been given to work in. A good memory for the table talk of whores is a great asset in life.

No doubt the colonel explained it all to me when I won the place off him but I must have been too excited to take it all in. It was built on the lines of the most opulent Parisian brothel you ever saw. Well, I don't actually know how many you've seen; it certainly outshone the most opulent *I* ever saw – and I've seen a hundred or more in my time.

The general effect in the corridors and public rooms was of a harem, as I have said; but the individual bedrooms – a dozen in all – each reflected a different taste. One was straight out of Versailles; one from a millionaire's yacht; one a baronial castle; one the silken tent of a desert sheikh with a passion for divans, curiously shaped footstools, and a warehouse load of silken cushions . . . there was even a railway carriage that rocked on springs while a painted landscape scrolled past outside; also a servant's garret, complete with threadbare blankets and patched linoleum – all lovingly reconstructed, like a photographer's setting, inside a large marble chamber.

The girls, of course, opened every drawer and cupboard in sight, squeaking with delight at everything they found – harem costumes, naughty French underwear, frilly petticoats, lacy corsets and bust bodices . . . garments that were capable of every degree of revelation and concealment . . . silk stockings and suspenders, ribbons, bow, drawstrings. At first it was the sort of laughter that said, "How could girls bring themselves to wear such things," but gradually the realization dawned on them that the question was more than pertinent to their own situation here; then the laughter shifted subtly toward a would-I-dare, would-you-dare kind of embarrassment.

Miss Parkin remained a little apart; at one stage, when the laughter was its height, I took her aside. Eve raised an eyebrow. I sought to reassure her with a wink.

"Listen," I told Miss Parkin when we were alone in the corridor outside, "if you want no part in this, my dove, I'll quite understand. If it's a question of money . . ."

"Don't you want me?" she asked quickly.

"I can hardly keeep my thoughts off you. I look at you and go weak with desire. But what do *you* wish in all this?"

She took my face between her hands and pressed a soft kiss on my lips, a kiss that was cinnamon and spice and that marvellous musky aroma only redheads exude. "I'm ready now," she said. She was shivering, too.

She had studied well for the part, and though I knew she was probably as false as Eve, I had to close my eyes to break her spell. Such is my uncomplaining slavery to that snug nowhere between their legs! "Later," I whispered.

"Soon," she insisted.

I nodded. "And one other thing. I'll treat you no differently from the others – in any way. You understand me?"

She smiled.

"But don't tell them yet." I tapped my forehead. "An idea is beginning to take shape up here. But, for the moment, I'll pretend to treat you the way they'd expect. Funny people, the middle classes. But then we – the aristocracy and the workers of the world – have always known that, haven't we?"

She laughed and hugged me again. "Poke me before *her,"* she begged. "At least do that."

When we returned to the morning room, Nimrod brought us sherry and biscuits. I insisted Miss Parkin should join us, though she still chose to sit slightly apart. We toasted each other in welcome. Then I explained to all four of them what I had already told my two founder scholars - that if they worked hard, played hard, and lived up to the best traditions of the dear old alma mater, they should all graduate into a decent marriage among the aristocracy.

"Even Parkin?" Miss G- asked.

"Even her," I insisted.

When they were all unpacked and settled we repaired once again to the morning room, where plush chairs served as our academy benches, and escritoires and occasional tables as writing desk. They were each to compose a brief essay explaining why they were so especially qualified for a life of erotic pleasure. Miss G- complained at once that it was all very well for me to go peeking and prying into their private lives and thoughts - but what about mine? Why didn't I write a corresponding essay on: "Why I am so amazingly qualified to teach the Arts of Venus"? I told her she was plainly going to make a splendid pupil. But I complied readily enough with her suggestion. Indeed, I have incorporated most of my little essay in an earlier portion of this book - in between the undoing of Eve's first button and of her second.

There follows a selection from their responses.

MISS G-: I did not fully understand that the life you offered in your advertisement was one of amorous pleasure. Parkin told me something of the sort on the train up to London and it came as quite a shock.

(Don't be deceived by her, by the way. She's not out for pleasure at all. Money is the only thing that kindles *her* desires.) I confess I almost took the next train back to Scotland but, as she pointed out, even if I didn't understand what was being offered, everyone else did and no one would believe I didn't. I have therefore burned my boats and might as well go ahead with it. I'm ready to be persuaded. That's all I can say.

As for amorous pleasure, I know nothing about it. I do not consider my person particularly well adapted for whatever it may involve. Generally, I have given the subject no thought whatever. You have a long, hard road ahead of you with *me*, my lord.

ABIGAIL: I'm fed up with so called "young gentlemen" (and many who are not so young, too) pushing themselves up against me in dark doorways here and there about the house, begging for a kiss and stealing a grope and always hoping to go all the way with me. It was fun for a time or two, or three, but when they fix a kid in you, they don't want to know you, ask any of the other maids.

Also I'm fed up with yes Miss G–, no Miss G–, whatever you say Miss G–, and working all hours, and being paid no more that £40 a yr for it all. I reckon if I was taught the Arts of Love properly, by a True Gentleman who knows what's what, I could do pretty well for myself by the time I'm ten yrs older – and so be my own mistress for the rest of my life.

As for "Amorous Pleasure," well, I'm not setting my sights on that – not for myself, anyways. But if I can dish it out for the Gentlemen by the long ton, I know I'd be rewarded in like measure. So that's why I talked Miss G– into joining me. (Don't be taken in by her icy manner, by the way. She's as hot as a goat for it, underneath. Not that she knows it herself, mind. Which is why she's still a virgin.)

WILHELMINA: It was the vicar's daughter, Leonora Jenkins, who first introduced me to the pleasures of Venus. I boarded with them when my parents went on a tour of America. We shared the same bed and had not been in it two minutes before she asked if I wanted to feel the most exquisite pleasure imaginable. Of course, I said yes, and she at once drew off my nightgown and, she being already *au naturelle*, insinuated her thigh between mine, right up against my fork, whereupon she began making the muscle go hard and soft. Meanwhile she suckled on my nipples, which were still tiny – and yet, as I soon discovered, were furnished with all the sensations of delight that a full-grown woman might enjoy.

I will not call it "the most exquisite pleasure imaginable" – not that first night, anyway. But it surely was pleasing enough for me to want more, which I got a-plenty over the weeks that followed. I believe there is an instinct in people, all people, men, women, boys, and girls, that tells them what to do in these matters, entirely without instruction. A man and a woman reared in total ignorance of amorous pleasure, and finding themselves marooned together on a remote island, would nonetheless know exactly what to do when the time came. And so it was with Leonora and me when our time came – which was almost every night.

No, the word "almost" is a lie. During the year we shared that joyful bed we found ecstasy together every single night. We soon progressed from the crude stimulus of our thigh muscles to the sweetly tormenting delights of our fingers, practising first on ourselves and then applying our discoveries to each other . . .

After six months, entirely without knowing *why* we were doing these things and never for one moment suspecting it might have anything to do with boys or venery – two subjects of which we knew nothing, in any case – Leonora had devised an ingenious contraption composed of part of a discarded bicycle handlebar and an ordinary candle, held on with straps taken from old pairs of drawers and corset laces. With the help of this we were able to take turns to lie upon each other and perform what I now know to be the act of kind. At the time we thought of it as just one further refinement in our armoury of mutual pleasures . . .

The most curious thing, as I look back on that time, is that we did not discover the pleasure of mutual licking of each other's privities until our last few weeks together. All the more curious in that we began with a mutual suckling of each other's nipples!

Another odd fact is that despite my entirely feminine introduction to amorous pleasure, my desires are now fastened almost exclusively on men and I know the same is true of Leonora, for we have discussed it quite recently. That is why I was attracted by that advertisement which my parents took such peculiar pains to hide from me. And that is why I feel I am more suited than most girls to a life of amorous pleasure, for though I had never yet lain with a man before last night, that single experience has persuaded me I am shaped in both body and mind for the frequent exercise of my endowments.

[*These essays, being in the girls' own handwriting, are naturally on separate pieces of paper. Somewhere here, I feel, there must surely have been a sheet in*

Hornington's own hand commenting on the gulf between Wilhelmina's daring coyness of the previous night and this audacious piece of fiction. If she truly had been dildoed by Leonora, she was surely taking a mighty chance in promising that if he pricked her she would bleed! The most assiduous search has failed to reveal it. However, there is, or rather was, a comment in pencil in the margin, which seems to be in our schoolmaster's hand and which someone was annoyed enough to erase. Modern science has restored the message: "I read the original in 'Vicarage Venus', but you have made it more personal and charming." – FR]

EVE: "An unmarried girl should have her name printed in smaller type below that of her father on one of his cards . . ."

"If a caller turns down the corner of his or her card, it is taken as a sign that he has included the daughters of the house in his call and is willing to entertain a return call by them upon him or her . . ."

"Always put on your gloves in your bedroom. Never let the servants – or anyone else, for that matter – see you drawing them on as you descend the stairs . . ."

"A lady should not bow to another with whom she was only conversed in a casual way at, say, a garden party given by a mutual acquaintance of theirs. Such meetings do not constitute a basis for an acquaintance . . ."

These wise old preachments – and a million like them – must be among the most inflammatory inducements to amorous sin ever devised. What normal young girl, after a mere fifteen minutes' exposure to them, does not wander in her thoughts? I know I do. In fact, I have endured those powerful seductions so many times I can enumerate their every tiny step.

First there comes a strange melting sensation that seems to have no focus in my body but that rather flickers through my veins like the leaping flame of a Romany fire. Bit by bit it gathers, palpitating in my chest, billowing in my stomach, and coursing like new blood in that secret fastness between my navel and my knee. I marvel at my outer calm even as my throat turns dry, my limbs grow feeble, and the roaring imperative in my ears drowns out my would-be teacher's voice. It is all I can do not to tear off my clothes and hurl myself at the first thing in trousers – which, had I not seen your announcement and letters to my parents, dear Hardy, is probably what I should have done before now.

In fact, it was my parents' willingness to allow me to accompany you (for a consideration of at least £2,000, it is true) that opened my eyes. They, the dear good kind sweet upright people (no girl could wish for better, I'm sure) – they would never have dreamed of letting me go into a life of degradation and misery, for anything less than £2,000.

I *come* with their blessing, you might almost say.

I read through these efforts while they dressed for luncheon. Where, I wondered, had dear little Eve hidden her memories of her father's lecherous partner and his erotic library? It seemed it was to be a new fiction each day with her. And each night, as well, I wondered?

We spent that afternoon at the zoo, trying to catch the animals at it – which I thought might put our studies in a wider, if not exactly nobler, perspective. But it was cold and we had little success, animals being only human in that respect. (Or do I mean humans are only animal? A topic for an advanced essay, perhaps.)

When we returned, all they could think of was a hot fire, toasted muffins, tea, and a bath.

And all I could think of, having lusted after her most of that afternoon, was sweet little Abigail – whom I extracted from the company, or from her customary place on its fringe, and took outside, saying it was high time we found her some suitable quarters in the house.

She was not deceived. She knew her moment had arrived and she fell into such a shivering she could hardly stand.

"Which room would you like for our pleasures?" I asked.

"I've been desperate for the touch of you all afternoon," was all she replied.

"Don't! I couldn't even begin to describe my longing for you. What about the imitation servant's garret?"

"No! Have *her* there – Miss G–."

"The railway carriage then?"

"Yes!"

We raced directly to it and I pressed the button that set the electric motors turning. It was very realistic once you were inside; only the clicketty-clack of the tracks was missing.

"We have to do this properly," I told her. "We're two strangers who happen to be travelling the same line. Everyone else got out at the last station. Now we find ourselves alone together. D'you prefer 'back to the engine', by the way?"

"Facing," she said.

We took our respective seats. "We've been giving each other the glad eye for some time," I added.

She laughed. "Well that's no make-believe at least."

We gazed at each other. She lowered her eyes and

blushed. I looked at the passing landscape . . . and then back at her. She licked her lips. I bit mine and smiled, shyly at first, then with growing confidence. She lowered her eyes again but at once raised them.

"Pardon my addressing you when we have not been introduced," I said, "but do you not find it a trifle bright in here? I wonder . . . if I lowered the blinds . . .?" I gestured toward the corridor.

"It would be better, perhaps," she agreed. "Such rough people travel by train these days."

"Does the thought of them disturb you? Shall I bolt the door, too?"

"Oh, that would be so kind. I know I shall be safe with you."

When I had completed these tasks I turned back to her – only to find she had loosened the top two buttons of her blouse. "You do not object?" she asked hastily. "Only it is so very stifling in this compartment. I wonder you can keep that heavy jacket on all – and your waistcoat, good heavens!"

She began to peel off a pair of imaginary gloves – so perfectly that I swear I half glimpsed them coming away. "We should introduce ourselves," she said. "I am Lady Abigail Parkinson-Smythe – of the Selkirk Parkinson-Smythes, don't you know." She stretched out her hand. Her imitation of a grand dame was flawless.

"Ah, my lady," I said ruefully. "I am but humble Roger Horn, manservant to Colonel Trotter, the owner of this railway." I took her hand nonetheless and raised it with trembling fingers to my lips.

She shivered, too. "Oh come, Roger, I think all those old class distinctions are hopelessly outmoded, don't you? After all, under these fine clothes I am . . ." She faltered.

"Yes, my lady?"

"Call me Abigail, do. I am but a woman, I meant to say. As you, I feel sure, are every inch a man?"

"Every inch," I confirmed.

Her bosom was heaving. "Oh!" She fanned her face. "What can cause this heat?" She fiddled ineffectively with two more buttons and gave up. "How useless I am! I usually have my maid to do all that."

I fell to my knees before her. "Oh, my darling Abigail, I am already consumed by jealousy for the creature. But if one humble servant may stand duty for another . . .?" I put a hand to the recalcitrant buttons and eased one free, then the next, then the next . . .

"She's not humble," she replied, but her voice was straying. A dreamy quality descended on her. "Lady's maids these days . . . they're all . . . Roger! Should you be doing this to me?"

"Not unless you're also going to do it to me, Abigail." I offered the equivalent buttons upon my own shirt for her fingers to pluck – which suddenly became as adept as a pickpocket's. Moments later we were both stripped to our waists – or she would have been were it not for the impediment of a delicate bust bodice, held by an elasticated band below her breasts.

She expected me to lift it off her but I was lost in wonder and adoration of her skin and those large, pale freckles. Oh, she was so fair and fine and delicate, so slender, so graceful in every movement as she slipped her hands behind her, between her shoulder blades, and there released her little bodice. It fell, just as far as her nipples, but she pinned it under her arms to prevent a complete revelation of those charms. Her eyes challenged me to take it from her.

I hooked a finger around the material, in the cleft between her breasts, and pulled it slowly free. They were superb, flawless in every detail – soft, delicate, trembling, with their dark nipples standing out like cones; and they, too, were lightly freckled! It is always a moment of magic to me, to discover that a fresh girl, in her nakedness, is formed and furnished precisely as nature and my experience with a thousand of her sisters had taught me to desire. Each is uniquely herself, yet all are made for our (by which I mean her and my) ecstasy.

How I nuzzled and suckled those shapely bosoms! I showered them with my kisses – and her neck and shoulders, her blushing cheeks, her comely lips, her finely chiselled nose, her pale brow . . . and all the while my senses were stabbed and drowned with that cinnamon-musk that flowed from every pore of her delectable young body.

She meanwhile was pick-pocketing my fly buttons apart and reaching inside for the great giver of our pleasures, hot and beating in his silken lair. The touch of eager, girlish fingers around that staff of life is indescribably sweet to me . . . their gentle grip, half fearful, half adoring. Even their feverish clumsiness is a pleasure sharp and poignant.

She took my hands off her breasts and pushed them down to her skirts. "I feel a sort of *scream* inside me down there," she murmured. "I shall have a fit soon unless . . . oh, be quick!"

While I thrust her skirts up, she unbuttoned them at her side; her petticoats were laced to them, so they came free of her, too. She was naked underneath and I found myself staring directly at her open sea, briny and brimming with her desire. I lowered my lips to her girlish bud, but she pulled my head away. "Later," she moaned. "Don't wait now."

Ah, the smell off her! It was musk and vixen and all things wild and free. She wriggled forward, bringing

Cupid's furrow to the edge of the seat; there, too, she could spread her thighs wide and offer it to me, pouting large, begging my entry. Her pearly flesh curled down on either side of her gaping honeypot, framing it like a pair of fingers, holding it open. I pushed my Lad against those eager lips and slowly pushed the old tickletail inside her, feeling gently for the resistance of her maidenhead. There was none. I went in – to the hilt of me and to a cry of joy from her.

She fell forward upon me. I thought she had passed out, but it was just to squirm against me and press her bosom to mine. When I took those two dainty young orbs in my hands and began to squeeze and caress her nipples she rose effortlessly to her first thrill. After that she sat almost perfectly still, mouth open, gaze a million miles away, scarcely breathing at one moment, gasping in extremis the next. Thus I brought her back to it again and again. Finally I let myself go and, thrusting as hard and as fast as I could, poked us both up to a final climax together.

And that was when I looked up and saw three reproachful pairs of eyes, three otherwise adorably young and girlish pairs of eyes, trained – if you'll forgive the word – upon us. The cyclorama landscape was cycling away behind them. I looked in alarm at Abigail. But she was grinning broadly. She wriggled and turned until she was kneeling before me and presenting her lovely young *derrière* for a second helping of my great girlometer. What could I do? It was such a very sweet and charming *derrière*. And my great girlometer was sure he had not yet got the full measure of her.

[*Here occurs the most annoying of the gaps in Hornington's papers – which I explain in my Postscript. Every page from this point on refers to the*

Academy as containing not four but six young girls. The two extras were Jonquil Davis and Fleur Duclos. Jonquil was twenty and haled from Anglesea, where her father was an excise man; Fleur, twenty-one, was her French maid. Jonquil, to paraphrase a number of hints and clues from later in the manuscript, was a buxom, frizzy redhead and extremely well-endowed. In one of Hornington's less inspired rambles on sex, which I have cut, he observes that Jonquil, though out of her teens, was in many ways the most childlike of all "his" girls; sex, which she had only ever talked about and sniggered about – but not, like the other five, thought about at all – was just a jolly-sounding game to her. Fleur was the exact opposite. Of average height, with short, dark, curly hair, she had the most compelling blue eyes, the colour of sapphires and quite riveting. Her figure, which was encased in a most elegant sheath of silk, was, in our hero's words, "mouth-watering. I felt sure she was no virgin but the very sight of her gave me a thousand reasons to overlook the deficiency."

The manuscript resumes with Miss G–'s induction into the magic and mystery of sexual pleasure, either on the evening of Hornington's session with Abigail in the fake railway carriage, or shortly after. – FR]

I chose Miss G– next and took her to the imitation servant's garret. I could feel an enormous resistance radiating from her towards me, like blasts of heat from a furnace – except that these blasts were colder than the coldest ice.

However, it is very hard for a virgin girlie of nineteen not to be desirable. She may fume and sweat with her inexperience; she may stammer and blush and make foolish remarks and drop things and just sit there loathing herself and you and whoever invented *la différence*, but nothing can detract from the youthfulness of her figure, the bloom on her skin, or the clarity of her eye. And above and beyond all that is the knowledge that no earlier Samson has thrust apart the white marble pillars of that universal temple where Adam fell and all his sons must follow.

A thousand generations of male inheritance came to buoy me up with whispered promises that mine would be the first flesh to waken hers to its destiny. There behind the veil of her maidenhead lay that old familiar glutton; there in that ravenous maw lurked a myriad nerves, all a-tremble to ring out their shattering of joy; there was her secret fuse, primed and ready to shake her with intimations of paradise. And here is my one-eyed Polyphemus, a complementary investment of blood and gristle; his nerves have thrilled times beyond number to those same joys, and each time I thought it an unique new beginning. And now I – no other man in all the world but I – am privileged to bring our vibrant, trembling organs together and touch off that cataclysm of ecstasy.

We were both still fully clothed. I looked at her lank, gawky body, whose forms were more guessed at than seen, and tried to remember the last time I had got inside a girl who started by resisting me. There must have been such occasions but I could not actually recall one. Yet I was astonished at the erotic power of her refusal; my desire to possess her immediately and at all costs evaporated as, with some misgiving I must admit, I gave myself up to this novel pursuit of what I was sure I'd gain in the end.

I took her by the shoulders and bore her gently backwards onto that imitation servant's bed. She offered no direct resistance – I mean, she put up no actual fight; but she lay there stiff as a plank and trembling like an aspen. I stretched myself at full length beside her and asked her to tell me something about her love affairs.

She said nothing.

"I truly would like to hear of them," I added.

"What sort of things?" she asked grumpily, half of her no doubt thinking this a mere postponement of her torture, the other half welcoming it for that same reason.

"Whatever comes into your head."

After a silence she said, "What 'love affairs' can be a respectable young girl of nineteen be expected to have? Really, I don't know what world you live in."

"A happier one than yours."

She gave out a single, mirthless laugh. "Well, that wouldn't be difficult."

"I can't believe that no young men came a-courting. I've been to Edinburgh myself. I know what goes on behind those prim, respectable granite façades. You've got the hottest blood in the kingdom in that city."

She laughed, despite herself, but soon returned to her dour old threnody. All her brushes with courtship, she claimed, had been miserable. "My mother says I only choose men who'll make me miserable. She says that really I want nothing to do with love; I just want the men to break it off and leave me inconsolable, because that's easier than shouldering the responsibilities that come when love ripens into marriage."

"And is your mother right?" I asked.

"How do I know? I always pick rotters, I know that. I agree with her to that extent. But why? I wish I knew."

"Why did you respond to my advertisement, then?"

"Because I thought at least there'd be no nonsense about love in the arrangement. You'd pay me so much. You'd tell me what to do. I'd pretend to enjoy it . . ." She abandoned the train of thought. "I don't know why. I didn't think very clearly I suppose. I just make a mess of everything I ever touch."

I thought it curious that every girl except Abigail had initially given me one set of reasons or arguments for her decision to seek me out – and then immediately contradicted them at the second time of asking.

"D'you want to leave again? Go home?" I asked.

"I suppose you'd be relieved."

"I'd be heartbroken, G– – truly, I mean it. There is something in you I find immensely appealing."

"You like messes, do you? I nearly puked just now. You'd have loved that!"

"You're not a mess."

"Ha ha!"

"Honestly you aren't. Your emotions are – no point denying it."

"What's the difference between my emotions and me? I don't understand."

I risked reaching out a finger and giving her arm a gentle tickle. "Like to find out?"

"What d'you suppose you could do?" she sneered.

I burst out laughing, which was a mistake – but then I was a stranger in that land myself. I laughed because she was so randomly predictable – that is, after she had done or said anything you could say, "How typical of her!" – even though, in advance, you had no idea what might happen. "Sorry," I said hastily, feeling her grow all tense and remote again. "To tell the truth, old thing – I haven't the foggiest notion what to do. What a wonderful teacher I've turned out to be, eh?"

"Yes, *what* a teacher!" She repeated the sneer; but I said it first.

"I'll tell you one thing that stands out," I added.

"Apart from old Polyphemus down here! It seems to me that you've been surrounded all your life by people who know beyond a shadow of a doubt what's best for you - and yet they haven't exactly been a howling success. Perhaps it's time you tried someone like me? An hereditary idiot who hasn't the first idea?"

I thought she might laugh but she burst into tears. I took her arms off her face and gripped them hard - actually, much too hard. I just wanted her to stop crying. She stopped all right.

But the transformation that came over her was astonishing. Her lips parted in that familiar, dreamy smile which I had seen in so many girls lying on their backs with their eyes closed. She gave out one long sigh of contentment. "Oh yes!" she whispered.

It caught me completely off my balance. I heard myself squawking like a virgin youth, "What does that mean - oh yes?"

"Hurt me," she begged.

And I, the arrogant, cocksure fool, refused.

My Dream - by G- H-

He drove me before him, up to the servant's attic, telling me all the way that my work had been slovenly, that I had been surly and impudent, and that now I should pay the penalty. I begged him to dismiss me without character or reward but to spare me those cruel whippings he had wreaked in the past upon my poor tortured skin. I told him last time he had been so severe with me that my heart had stopped and I thought I should die. I asked did he want to finish on the gallows for such an undeserving slut as me?

He paid me not the slightest heed but his merciless eye quelled me to silence and I saw that, even if death on the gallows was to be his punishment for this night's work, he would not abate mine by a single stroke of the many implements of torture he kept prepared for my chastisement. Even now my piteous cries still ring in my ears. Oh, how I begged him to show some slight tenderness towards me, some little act of mercy! Yet even now, when I am awakened from that nightmare, I can still see that relentless glint in his eye, and I feel once again that I am doomed, bereft of all help or possibility of escape.

I might scream at the top of my voice but who is there to hear me in this desolate Highland brae? I could take to my heels and run, for I am not held in chains – not yet, at least – and the doors are all unbarred. But I recall the last time I tried anything so foolish as that. He laughed like the Lord of Hell and saddled his great black horse and unleashed his mastiffs and harried me over glen and burn till dawn came and I sank exhausted in the heather. In my soul I bear the marks of those hounds' teeth about me still. In the blear light of that ghastly dawn I had gaping wounds that stained the whole loch red; yet they did not save me from even the smallest of the punishments from which I had tried to flee. He bore me back, trussed me tight, and yet another of my day-long, nightlong ordeals began.

Now, on this night when I must endure it all again, I can hear his hounds whimpering in the kennels. That evil black stallion kicks and stamps in its stall. Their memory drives me before him, his unchained prisoner, "free" to run.

I stand within the door, my eyes downcast. There is no need to look about me for I know every inch of this room by now. From the depths of my despair I have studied it, brick by brick, thinking that if my eyes could only possess one part of it with sufficient intensity, the rest of me, my sentient flesh, might follow, leaving the mere shell of my skin to accept his worst. But the trick, if such even exists, has always eluded me. It will elude me again tonight. I know it now before the first shock of pain has racked me, just as I know how desperately I shall soon be casting about, hoping for that magic to work this time. That is why I do not look about me yet; I do not wish to be reminded of all those past failures.

That knowledge is part of the terror. I know I shall grow desperate to escape my tormented flesh. I know I shall fail. I know this demon at my heels will hurt me to within an hairsbreadth of oblivion. I know he will stop before that mercy overwhelms me. I know he will revive me with some absurd little kindness. I know he will begin again. I know that only the dawn – or the satisfaction of his unmentionable lusts – will save me at the last.

Dawn! How unwelcome to the poor, exhausted servant girl in any night but this! Yet now I would give a queen's ransom and all my hope of salvation to see it already here. But how many stinging lashes of the whip, how many cuts of those vicious canes – several of which he will break in breaking me – how many licks of the cat, how many assaults of that cruel piledriver which rears from between his thighs . . . how many of these must I endure before the sun returns? I dare not even guess at their number.

"Sweet child," he tells me in a voice that would melt any young girl's heart. "You know how deeply you have vexed me with your wicked ways?"

"Yes, master." It is no good to deny it for the punishment is then swifter and more terrible still.

"You know it is a charity, then, to chastise you for your wickedness? For how else may you hope to reform?"

"I know it, master, and I thank you from the bottom of my heart."

"And are you truly ashamed?"

"I am ashamed beyond all measure, my dear, good master."

"Come now, G–, I think you cannot be telling the truth. For if you were truly ashamed and if you truly desired to be washed clean of your wickedness, what would you be saying to me? What would you be begging me to do?"

"To chastise me, my good, sweet master."

"How?"

"Without mercy, sir. And so I do. I beg you now – whip me without mercy, flog me within an inch of my life. Revive me with thumbscrews and hot coals. Unflesh my ribs. Do this, dear master, out of love for me – and show me that love, even in the spate of your righteous anger . . . that love which every orifice in my body already craves with . . ."

"Well, well. That is good enough. Since you desire this just and rightful punishment so ardently let us begin. And think not of the pain it gives me to use you so. Think only that I do it for the good of your everlasting soul. Let us kneel and pray."

His prayer is obscene and I cannot repeat it here. When it is done I am almost faint with apprehension. My flesh, knowing only too well the torments to come, cannot hold still. My stomach is falling, falling, forever. I breathe in without breathing out, then in again, then again, until I know I shall burst – and still I fall short of breath. He has to lift and half-carry me, shivering like a leaf, to the spot where my torture always begins.

He raises my skirts and slips off one of my stockings, kissing my exposed limb as each portion is revealed. "Poor flesh!" he whimpers. "My heart bleeds for it already. The horrors it is about to taste!"

With the stocking he binds my wrists in a repeated

figure-eight that does not deprive my hands of blood – for bloodless flesh cannot feel. Then he drops a hook from the ceiling and with it raises my arms above my heard – tightening the rope to the point where I must stand on tiptoe or risk pulling my shoulders out of joint. One by one he lifts my skirts and pins them to my dress, between my shoulder blades. At last I feel the cold air upon my bared posteriors – and if I didn't, there would be his gasp of joy to confirm it.

Now begins his first game. The one with the whip.

Before me are several tall looking glasses in which, no matter what angle he may come at me, I can see his every move. It is a short-handled whip such as lion tamers use. The crack of its lash can be placed with hairsbreadth accuracy – no doubt you have seen circus artistes demonstrate this when they flick the tip off a lighted cigarette held between the assistant's lips, and all without harming a hair of her head. It is now my master's pleasure to deploy that skill upon me.

With the crack of that lash he will disrobe me entirely, by lashing at the buttons and breaking them or their thread. But the trick is this: he will lash at the button, not where it is now, but where it will be *if* I spot his movement in time and *if* I squirm out of his way to the limit of my tethered arms. And, since this would be poor sport if repeated without variation, every now and then, and quite unpredictably, he will aim at my posteriors a crack that no amount of squirming will enable me to escape.

Such evasions would be hard enough in full daylight and with my master in his everyday clothes. But in that dark hell-hole, with my master all in black like the executioner of old, and what feeble light there is trained onto my face, I have to rely more on my knowledge of his fiendish nature than on anything I might see. Indeed, all I can see most of the time is that great, thick ramrod beneath his navel. When it sways in a certain manner, which I know of old by now, he is drawing back his arm; when it gives a little pulse of delight, the lash is about to descend. No virgin child-bride of the Orient ever stared with more fascinated horror at the implement of her subjugation than I at that gorged and bloated cracksman of his.

It lurches. I leap. And the first unbelievable stab of pure pain screams through my body, radiating from my bottom. It is a terror no familiarity can dull, that first explosion of suffering. The assaulted flesh, even far from the seat of the hurt, takes fright, swoons, loses control, sweats, fumes, and trembles all anew. Oh, how ardently I squirm thereafter! How I writhe this way and that, to the limit of my sinews and beyond, to escape a second lashing as fierce as that first!

My writhing bottom, all girlish and vulnerable in the soft light of the candles, so inflames his lust that, after some twenty lashes - all of which I have evaded but the first - he leaps forward, flicks the leather snake around my belly, pulls me onto that great, hairy gristle, and plunges it to the hilt in me, ramming away until I cry out in my torment.

He leaps back in a fury, for it is an inviolate rule that when he favours any orifice of my tortured body with a visitation of that throbbing bowsprit, I am to moan in ecstasy and beg him never to cease - though in truth it is so vile a slug that when it comes at me I'd almost swear I longed again for the whip or cane. He lashes me - once, twice, thrice - those cuts I cannot evade. Surely I have never endured such a pain as this before? I forget to squirm beyond the reach of his next lash, at one of my buttons. For a moment I pass into happy oblivion.

He stops at once. When I recover, never having lost consciousness entirely, I am hanging limp at the rope's end while he is kneeling behind me, caressing the backs and insides of my thighs, showering kisses on my crimsoned bottom, and begging me remember he does it for my good, for my good alone. Then he returns to his place, picks up the whip, and lays it onto me afresh.

Countless lashes later, all but twenty of which he allows me to evade (for the game thus early is to exhaust me rather than fill my flesh with the swift oblivion of pain), the last buttonhole is breached and the last shred of my decency falls at my feet. Then with a whoop of delight he leaps at me once more and breaches that hole for which there is no button. A respite, you might think? A moment of pleasure to sharpen the tortures to come?

Alas, not so. In that unspeakably evil man, my master, even that flesh is a dealer of pain. In other men, and with other girls than I, it is an object of veneration and joy; in him, in me, it is the very executioner of all that could be called joy. From that vile and violent truncheon he radiates through my innards the essence of woe and affliction. Yet I must sigh, and murmur my ecstasy in his ear, and beg him go on and on – harder, ever harder . . .

Miss G– looked up from her reading aloud and said, "That's as far as I got."

There was a groan of frustration from all the other girls – except Jonquil, who looked around at the rest in total bewilderment. I had been watching them keenly during Miss G–'s recital and was amazed at the transformation that had swiftly overtaken them. They resented her at the beginning, because they knew I had not touched her – or not in the sexual meaning of the word. (I didn't tell them; she did – immediately and with the inverted pride of the person who knows she's born to lose and fail.) Yet within the first two or three paragraphs they became aware that she was about to describe a sexual experience that none of them could match, dream or no dream.

Oddly enough, I believe the only person there who did not think of it as sexual, was Miss G– herself! Even Jonquil sniggered and hid her smile behind her soft, fleshy hand as she glanced at "teacher" to see how he was taking it. But to Miss G– it was too personal, too deeply felt, to have anything to do with sex – which she regards as something shallow, silly, and repulsive. Even the rapes her dream-master visits on her are carefully separated from real sexual experience, which, as she says, is for "other men with other girls than I".

"When was all this supposed to have happened?" Jonquil asked.

Miss G– merely stared at her in contempt.

The other four were still lost in a daze. The tale, or, more likely, the lugubrious relish with which Miss G– had told it, had undoubtedly left them excited. And because it was unfinished, their excitement was tinged with frustration, too. I observed them glancing slyly at one another, at first a little shamefaced – supposing that this response was theirs alone. Then came a recognition of it in each others' eyes – incredulous, accusing, delighted . . . all sorts of fleeting emotions in one swift parade. Yet still they wondered which would be first to admit it aloud.

I waited for that moment before I asked Eve what she had thought of it. For reply she turned to Miss G– and murmured – almost as if she were afraid to break some fragile spell, "How could you imagine such a thing? And make it so real?"

Miss G–, unused to compliments, gave an awkward shrug. "I've always been interested in torturers and things. It used to be highly respectable, you know? Archbishops and popes and even the mildest kings – they all had their tortures, who were honoured and revered."

"Actually," I said, speaking as offhandedly as I could manage, "dear old Trotter has left us a good stock of whips and canes – in the big trunk on the upstairs landing. Would any adventurous young miss like to learn what just a single lash on the bare posteriors actually feels like?"

They giggled too much, looked around at each other – also too much – and protested that they most certainly would not.

"Oh, well," I said, "it's not locked. If you want to experiment, just help yourselves."

"Would any adventurous teacher like to learn what he would so obviously love to teach?" Eve asked pointedly.

"With the greatest of pleasure!" I responded at once. "Go and choose your weapons – all of you if you like."

All they did was giggle once more; but the yeast was working.

"Well," I said in a conciliatory tone, "perhaps the pleasures of the grand old Marquis and of the poor dear Baron are a little too advanced for us as yet. So who else has an essay ready? As you've just seen – they needn't be finished to be absolutely fascinating." I looked around that circle of bright and charming eyes. "Abigail?"

She shook her head in frightened denial and clutched her schoolbook to her.

"Fleur?"

She smiled. "My English is not good. I'ave wrote 'im *en Français.*"

"The language of love," I said.

I managed a brilliant extempore translation at the time, of course; but here is a more polished version:

The Education of a French Courtesan – by Fleur Duclos

I am the eldest in a family of four girls and three boys. My parents are farmers in Normandy on some rather poor land in the Pays d'Auge. They should have stopped at three but my father was a passionate man and my mother made the best cider for miles. It was quite obvious that the farm would never support us all, much less provide dowries for so many girls.

Norman peasants are a practical race and my mother determined that the first of us girls to retain her pretty looks into the dawning of her womanhood would be sent to Paris to earn the marriage portions of herself and her sisters. In her case it was an easy decision to make and carry out because two of my aunts, her sisters, were *institutrices* – that is, they owned a small but select *maison de tolérance,* or bordel, in the Latin Quarter, near the house of M. Rodin. All the great men of France had been there. Gautier, Daudet, de Maupassant, Flaubert, Murger, Allais, Courbet . . . all were clients of my aunts. So was Balzac, but then every brothel in Paris could say the same of him. My aunt said when she was little – when the bordel belonged to her mother, she saw Balzac leaving the place one afternoon just as she was returning from school. He was with M. de Paty, the Prefect of Police. Oblivious of her the great writer put his hand under his vast, straggling beard and lifted it, pressing it to his nostrils and sniffing deeply. "Ah, those girls, Paty! Those girls!" he murmured. That commonplace little incident became the centrepiece of my dreams, the very target of my ambition. I wanted all the great gentlemen of Paris to spend their hour with me and then go out into the street and sniff their beards and lips and fingers and murmur, "Ah Fleur - ah, my dear, sweet Fleur!"

To prepare a girl for the life of a drab on the streets is the work of minutes. You give her enough absinthe to dull the sensitivities of any woman, expose enough skin to awaken those of any man, and push her out the door. But the education of a fine courtesan takes at least a year.

To begin with, the sale of her maidenhead will secure her dowry; and since, with the judicious use of pucker-water and well-schooled coyness, it can be *re*sold four or five times, it will secure her sisters' dowries, too. A year on her back will buy a large farm. Two years will stock it with the finest pedigree herd and fill the cupboards with linen. Three will add the silver and a good carriage. I was to begin at seventeen and work to this plan, finishing on my twentieth birthday, at which time I was still not too old to marry and I could moreover have my pick of Normandy's youth. So at sixteen my education commenced. (In every other house in Paris at that time, a girl would make her sacrifice at least one and more often two years younger than that. But my aunts, who were long in the trade, knew they could get much longer service out of their girls if they started them later. Their maidenheads might fetch less, but the profit over the years outweighed the loss many hundreds of times over.)

As far as my aunts were concerned, every lesson was aimed at those first few sales of my maidenhead; what happened thereafter was in the lap of the gods - or, as one of them said with a sly wink, "in *some* sweet young lap not too far from heaven." And for those initial sales they needed to achieve a delicate and subtle balance between charming ignorance and informed coquetry. Total ignorance would be disastrous; I might scream and scratch the gentleman and kick him where it would cost the return of his entire fee. Total understanding might be subtly worse, for I could act the wanton with my deflowerer and so deprive him of the joy of leading a virgin from innocence to ecstasy – which is what they pay so dearly to enjoy.

The men realize it is partly a trick, of course. They know that *some* of the young virgin's reluctance is her schooling, and so, too, is *some* of her later rapture. Ah, but how much? If her teacher has been thorough, the division between the heartfelt and the learnt-by-heart is quite invisible. That is why they count it money well spent, for men are the greatest romantics ever. They will travel the earth for a seamless performance and waste whole fortunes in its enjoyment.

Therefore, to preserve that essential innocence which would be half my bargain, they kept me, at first, strictly apart from the girls, The "house" was, in fact, two houses side by side; the bordel occupied all of the left hand one and the top two floors of the other; my aunts and I occupied the rest. I had my own room and my own maid, Hortense, a gaunt, plain girl from Alsace. My aunt said when she first came to them she would wash under the pump in the yard, never having seen a basin; and as for her other ablutions, she would take a spade into the shrubbery! Yet, despite her rough ways and her unprepossessing looks, gentlemen sometimes asked for her in preference to the beauties who were paraded in the salon for their choice. Hortense would go to them giggling and wiping her hands endlessly in her pinafore; and she would return with a dreamy sort of look in her eye. Often and often I begged her to tell me what they did, but she never would. However, that dreamy look and her triumphant smile were answers she could not withhold from me.

Her main function was to keep me in spotless linen and to make sure I bathed myself all over twice a day – something that did not come naturally to a girl of sixteen off a Normandy farm! At first it made me extremely uncomfortable. My skin felt as if it were peeled. But soon she was given creams and perfumes to rub into me, under my arms, down my back, over my belly, and between my thighs – and then my objections fell away.

There was nothing lascivious in this massage; it was far too early to embark upon that. My aunts' sole aim at that stage was to make me think of my body as something delicate, rare, precious – something to be pampered and petted – something of enormous value – intrinsic value, I mean, not commercial. That, too, came much later.

Looking back now I can hardly recall my state of mind at that time. I think I must almost have been two separate people cohabiting one girlish frame. Part of me knew why I was there, knew what all this preparation was for – and not in any abstract sense, either, for I already knew something of the intimate behaviour of men and women. I and my younger sister had larked about with my brothers, so I knew what male organs looked and felt like, both soft and hard. I had even held one in my mouth while it throbbed and emptied, though that was the only orifice in my body to have been so favoured by the time I went to Paris. So I was no little innocent babe! And yet I could go for days on end, pampering my body, enjoying my baths, wallowing in those lotions and perfumes – and never once would I consider the ultimate purpose of it all.

Thus my aunts succeeded in their first aim, which

was to make me regard my body as the most beautiful thing in my life – not as a spur to carnal lust nor as a means to gratify it, but as something warm, adorable cuddly, responsive, pleasurable, alive – *in itself*. If a *fille de joie* does not have that feeling about herself, she will never amount to much. Nor, I venture to say, will a wife, either.

All this while they were assiduous in keeping me to my religion. Every day my confessor came to me, set me my penances, heard my acts of contrition, and gave me absolution and the Holy Sacrament. I thought my aunts must be the most devout people in Paris; only later did I learn that they had sold my virginity to this very Monsignor, my confessor, for enough to furnish new plate to half a dozen churches; it was part of their bargain that he should hear my daily confession and follow my steady initiation to the sins of the flesh, one shyly whispered secret at a time. My naïveté amazes me now.

So there I lay, night after night, two silly little girls in one increasingly adorable body, the faux-naïve fool. Half of me knew that in the next-door house and in the rooms over my head, a dozen girls were spreading their relish for a hundred gentlemen every day. I could hear the screech of the bedsprings, the creaking of the floors. Their rhythms were part of the air I breathed, so that I got to know and wait for M'sieu Slow-and-steady, M Fast-and-furious, M Andante-moderato, M Crescendo, M Apache . . . I gave them all names and ticked off the days of the week by their encounters with my unseen, unknown sisters of joy. Yet the other half of me could no more relate these nightly buffetings to my own future than it could the other sounds of the Parisan night. For instance, I would hear a fiacre pass by and never once think of myself as climbing into one and saying to the driver, "Take me to so-and-so!" In the same way I would hear Monique or Céleste or Garence (I gave them all names, too) take gentlemen to their rooms, and yet I never once imagined myself in their position.

And so matters proceeded until some two months before my Great Sacrifice was to be made, which was to be on my seventeenth birthday. I attended my school, where the nuns said I was an example to all; I pampered my body and learned to adore the feel of it in silks and linen and fine clothes of every kind; I confessed my tiny sins and inflamed my Monsignor into a delirium – all without knowing it, of course; and I listened to the night music of the brothel as if it were the beating of distant drums in the rituals of a remote and obscure tribe.

And then my aunts sent Marianne to sleep with me.

Marianne was eighteen; she had been two years broken to the trade. This arrangement worked out well for all, because she had lately acquired a very rich lover who had become besotted with her. He spent two hours with her every afternoon and paid her and my aunts to keep her out of circulation as far as possible. The agreement was that she would only be sent into the salon if the choice of girls fell to two, or if some gentlemen requested her by name.

One of the first things I asked her was, "Why doesn't he pay enough to take you out altogether and keep you in a little nest of your own?"

"Because it excites him to torment himself," she explained. "He sits there every evening with his dull little wife, dreaming of me, and wondering, 'Is she with another man now? What are they doing this minute? Is he ramming his great *persuasif* into her sweet little *centre d'amour?* Is she moaning and sighing into his ears, pretending she can't get enough of him – as she does with me? Does she mean it when she's like that with me?' And so it goes on and on and on. *La carrousel d'amour!* He imagines me with half a dozen other men between his visits, and I must tell him all that we did, and how I felt, and how I had to pretend it was him just to make the thing bearable. And then we have to do those same things these imaginary men did to me, and I must tell him how superior he is. Honestly, Fleur, men are extraordinary!"

I asked her endlessly what it was like, the first time with a man. She gave me the answers my aunts had schooled her to give: It was delightful, one long delirium of pleasure that would leave me with the satisfaction of being a woman at last. Yet I could sense a certain reservation in her as she trotted out these pat replies, so I kept at her to give me more detail, to describe their movements like a choreographer and tell me at each little stage what she felt.

In the end she broke down. "Listen, little Fleur," she whispered one night, "if I were truly your teacher instead of your aunts' parrot, I should tell you something quite different. In fact, I should tell you the truth. Now if I do, will you promise never, never to tell them? They'd skin me alive if they ever found out. Promise?"

"But why should they get you to lie to me?" I asked.

"Because they think it's for the best. Because it's the traditional sort of comforting nonsense to tell little virgins like you. Because, although they are your aunts, they are also – and first and foremost – the *institutrices* of a very select high-number house with a certain reputation to maintain. Also they imagine that your deflowering will be almost over before you start saying to yourself, 'Just a moment – this is nothing like what I was promised!' But by then you will have one deliriously happy man squirting away between your legs, and the lies will have helped you earn your fee. That's how it worked with me, anyway."

"Then where's the harm in it?" I was not at all sure I wanted these comforting lies exposed.

"The harm comes in the following weeks, when you settle to regular work in the house. For months you've been fed a steady pap of golden promises. Reality simply can't live up to them. I agree – that first hour with a man is difficult. But the price they want you to pay for being helped through it is too high."

"What is the price?"

'Weeks or months of drab grey sadness as you dismantle your dreams and brace yourself for the daily shock of reality."

By now I was feeling awful. "Is it really so bad," I asked, "that only lies with carry me through it?"

"No!" she insisted. "That's the stupidity of it all. I think if you were told the truth, the simple truth, the shock would be less . . . in fact, I doubt if there'd be any shock at all."

"Tell me then," I urged. "I promise I won't say a word to my aunts."

"Not ever?"

"Never, never, never – promise. Tell me, moment by moment."

She shook her head in the dark. "No, it's not that sort of truth, little dove. 'First he does this, then he does that . . .' The truth is beyond all that. If you want it in one simple statement – the truth is that it's a very *animal* act. I don't mean bestial, now – though there are men who can make it so – but your aunts will shield you from them for at least your first year, I'm sure. No – it's, as I say, an amazingly *animal* act. That's what I remember thinking most vividly during my first time with a man. I had all this romantic nonsense in my head, the sort of stuff they want me to tell you. But he hadn't gone at me ten minutes before it all evaporated and I thought, 'Mon Dieu! I'm here on all fours just like a cow!' And d'you know what else? The same thought came back to me again and again during those awful depressing weeks afterwards, when I was being taken upstairs to be licked and stroked and prodded and poked by a dozen gentlemen every day. I kept telling myself, 'This is just an animal act.' And that helped me survive it – and now it's fine! Now I can even enjoy it sometimes."

I still wanted a picture though – and told her so.

She tried again. "The first thing is confusion." She reached over and tapped my breastbone. "In there. You're alone in a bedroom with this unknown man. You've never met him before in your life. You were only introduced five minutes ago and now he's already starting to take your clothes off and soon he'll do the most intimate thing possible with you. Part of you is excited by it, because that's the way girls are made, after all. But most of you is repelled at the very thought – because that's also the way girls are made. You want time, you'd like to think about it a bit more. You want to talk. Couldn't he just try kissing and cuddling this time, and come back tomorrow for the rest of it? But no. The bargain's struck. You've just seen more money change hands than you ever saw in your life – and half of it is yours. So now you have to perform your share of the bargain." She paused and asked, "Can you picture it now?"

I sighed. "All too clearly."

"Good. So when he comes near you and takes off some of his clothes the biggest surprise is the aroma of him. I don't mean a stink but . . . you know how stallions have a decided aroma, and bulls, and boars? And it's different from fillies and heifers and gilts?

Well, it's the same with men. There is a male aroma that is different from girls. Actually, that was the first thing that struck me when I entered the bordel – the aroma of girls. Perhaps I just notice aromas. Anyway, that was a big surprise on that night I sold my jewel – the aroma of males."

"And the second?"

"I don't remember much of what followed – or, rather, it was so like the next night and the next night and every other man on every other night since that it's all sort of merged. Yet I must have said and done all the right things, because he told your aunts afterwards that I had been superb. I must have helped him get out his tool. And then I must have stared at it with just the right mixture of adoration and alarm . . . and I must have been coy and eager in just the right proportions – but I honestly don't recall any of it."

"What, not even when he broke your hymen?"

"No. They warned me I might feel a little discomfort at that point but I think I was in such a daze. What I *do* remember is much later, towards the end, when I was on my back with my heels up beside his ears and him kneeling and poking his piledriver in and out of me pretty vigorously, and I could hear his groin and belly going slap, slap – really quite loud – against my bottom and the backs of my thighs, and the sharp little sticky noises it made with my juices – these are the things you never imagine in advance, the actual sound of it. And his getting short of breath as his excitement grew, and giving out little cries of pleasure, and me exclaiming, 'Oooh!' and 'Phew!' and then trying to disguise them as ejaculations of ecstasy, and both of us gleaming with sweat. And *that's* when it struck me – the one thing I do remember, most vividly – *What an animal act it all is!* So there – now you know the truth."

She was called back to the salon at that moment.

Most nights she was called into service once or twice, usually during the evening hours, while I was still awake, when trade was at its most brisk. After a time I began to tease her, pretending I was her rich lover and asking her in a jealous tone who she had been with, what did he look like, what did they do . . .?

At first she didn't think it at all funny, but then she used it as a means to further my education. She felt she had done enough to open my eyes; now it was time to give me a little encouragement so that I can understand that – like everything else in life – the way of the *fille de joie* is ninety percent dull, five percent disagreeable, and the rest good fun.

"Oh," she says, "he was a very handsome young officer from the Madeleine – the sort we girls dream about and go wild to secure."

My heart begins to beat faster. "And what did he do? Did he gaze deep into your eyes and make you feel . . ."

"He did this." She leans over and begins to kiss my shoulder, my neck, my ears. "Would you like to pretend you're me?" she asks. "And I'll be him?"

"Yes," I murmur. A wild palpitation seizes my heart; my breathing grows shallow and disordered as she continues running her lips up and down my neck. Although she is a woman – and I know she is a woman – she has somehow also become a man, a dashing young officer, and I long for him-her to kiss me on the lips.

Her hand steals across me, caresses my other shoulder. Her fingernails rake gently through my hair, sending shivers up and down my spine and into my very core. My pampered, adored, and perfumed body has been remade for just this encounter. I know this is probably a part of my aunts' carefully chosen curriculum for me. I know why this lovely sister has been sent to warm me; yet nothing can halt my abandonment to that most ancient delirium of all.

We are both naked between the sheets. My breasts are flushed with perspiration and my nipples itch like mad. When she moves her lips down and kisses them and sucks them in between her teeth, the madness spreads throughout my body. For a moment I feel the certainty of death, which invades me with shots of fire and ice and electricity.

"Now," she murmurs, knowing to what heights my pleasure has risen, "see how long you can stay there." And her fingers slip down between my thighs, where they rub and press and wriggle around my cleft in a thousand delightful ways - but never so as to endanger what she laughingly calls the most expensive square centimetre of skin in the entire Latin Quarter. For ten minutes she uses all her skill to keep me there, in that feverish ecstasy I had never before known.

Then she is called back to the salon, to do the same ritual all over again for another unknown gentleman, and I fall into the sweetest slumber. Her cunning was never to let me feel that it was *she,* another woman, doing this to me; always she presented these loving tricks as things I might expect a man to do.

But then, if I showed signs of overconfidence, or started talking in an altogether too blasé a tone, she would quickly find some means to whip up my fears. For instance, I once asked her if it was really only one square centimetre, that costly skin down there. I added that I had got my thumb inside to feel it gingerly, and the tip of my thumb I later measured at 1.6cm diameter - which gave it an area of twice what she had said. She, thinking this altogether too casual and sophisticated for a virgin of my tender years, responded that a typical diameter for the *flageolet* that would soon be making its own sweet music in that bosky hollow is *four* centimetres – and would Mlle Diderot like to calculate the area of that!

"Why, it is over *twelve* square centimetres," I told her, turning as pale as my own linen.

After that, it took many nights of skilful pleasuring with her fingers to get me back into a receptive frame of mind. And I still had nightmares in which all the men in Paris were walking around naked and without faces. Their only distinguishing features were their *bondons des filles* [*literally, "girl-bungs" – FR*], which were all shapes and sizes, but always erect and twitching. It was all confused with the idea of a drag hunt. My perfume – the aroma from between my legs – had been dragged through the streets, and now all those faceless men with their ardent *bondons* were following it up – literally up – to the room where I lay. The door would not lock and I had forgotten the words to make them go away.

And so, on the last day in October, two days before I was to take my *baccalauréate* in cardinal sin – or monsignorial sin, which is just as terrifying – I was in a state of near hysteria, both yearning for and dreading the experience.

Fleur laid down her exercise book. "And I'm afraid that's all," she said simply.

"Oooooh!" A huge, collective sigh of disappointment went up from the others. "Tell us! You don't need to write it down – just tell us what happened. What was he like? Was it awful or simply *divine* – hee hee!" . . . and so on.

"But there is nothing to tell," Fleur insisted. "That very evening when it was to happen my father arrived in Paris and was overjoyed to learn that I had not yet yielded up my jewel. His father – my grandfather, of course – had been the last surviving member of a tontine, which he had collected the previous week. Unfortunately the shock of it had killed him, so my father was now the inheritor of over a hundred thousand louis and there was no need for me to make this dreadful sacrifice."

"Awww!" The sense of let-down among them was heartrending. "That's two stories which just sort of petered out at their most exciting moment," Jonquil complained.

I promised I would get around to as many of them as possible that night and give them what compensatory comforts I could. But I could see one or two of them already beginning to exchange significant glances and it occurred to me that those two unfinished tales might yet turn out to be all for the best in their sentimental education. After all, here was a house built for erotic fantasy of every kind. Up on the landing were great trunks and boxes, full of canes, ticklers, and other aids to sensual delight. G–'s strange excursion into fantasy had suggested new horizons and Fleur's memoir had reminded them of the pleasures two uninhibited girls can find together. And above all, there was no one to say, "Stop, that's naughty!"

The situation was novel to me, too, but in a very different sense. I don't suppose I had ever consciously formulated the notion but always at the back of my mind had been this idea that a virgin girl is like the Sleeping Beauty. It needed the kiss of a man to awaken her to the pleasures of life. But now, watching my adorable young students and their entirely spontaneous responses to these rousing tales, I began to wonder how much they might discover on their own, with no help from me or any other man.

My thoughts were interrupted by a question from

Wilhelmina to Fleur. Ever the practical girl she asked: "And are you still a virgin?"

The French maid nodded all round but her smile was just for me.

Eve picked up the inquisition. "But if your family's so rich, why are you working here as a lady's maid?"

"My father said that, because I had been prepared to make such a noble sacrifice for my sisters, I should now have the chance to fulfil my life's true ambition. 'So what would you like to do?' he asked me. 'Money is no object.' I think my answer disappointed him, for my dream cost him very little beyond the fare to England and a few nice dresses."

"What was it? Do tell us," they chorused in frustration.

"But can you not guess? Why, it was to come to England and marry an English lord."

Her smile, which she beamed straight at me, was quite dazzling.

Of course I had to disabuse them all - and especially Fleur - of any stupid notion they might entertain that *I* might be the "member of the nobility" I had promised to find for them in marriage after their graduation from my humble academy. They smiled as if they knew better - all except Miss G–; her smile, I was pleased to notice, was one of understanding and approval. She really is the oddest mixture of immaturity and wisdom.

I was in a sort of Arabian costume and on my way to Fleur's room to take up the implications of that adorable smile when Miss G– flung her door wide. She must have been waiting for me, spying through a crack of an opening. She was fully dressed but her hair had been let down. "All alone?" I asked.

She nodded glumly.

"Won't any of the others . . ."

"I deserve it," she insisted.

"Why?"

She hung her head. "I've been a very naughty girl." She licked her lips, allowing her tongue to linger a moment there. I don't think the gesture was conscious.

"You know what happens to naughty girls?" I asked.

Her eyes fell. She nodded.

I sighed and took a step towards her. "Oh, G–, if only you knew how much pain it gives me to have to do this – far more, indeed, than it will cause you."

"Please don't hurt me too much," she begged. She was so immersed in her . . . what shall one call it – was it a dark compulsion or a charming fantasy? Anyway, she was so immersed in it that I could not tell whether this was a genuine request or part of the preliminaries she found necessary. The words "too much" were an interesting stage direction.

"Very well," I replied, still tight-lipped and unsmiling. "This time – but only this time – I shall spare you the worst of what would be a just and terrible punishment. I shall not use the whip, nor the birch, nor even the cane. I shall spank you with the flat of my hand."

"Oh, please no?" she begged as she ran happily back into her room – the mock servant's garret. "Don't spank me, please. Please, my dear, dear master? I beg you." She drew forth a chair and placed it for me to sit.

"What's this?" I asked.

She looked crestfallen. "I'm sorry, my lord. I assumed that, as this is my first punishment at your hands you'd put me over your knees, raise my skirts and petticoats tenderly and slowly to throw me off my guard, caress my bare posteriors with loving gentleness to lull me still further, and then sting me when I least expected it. Perhaps a dozen times but always caressing me in between to make the next one worse."

"Oh, did you, indeed?" I waited for more orders.

"Yes." She pushed me gently down into the chair. "And then if I repeated my transgressions tomorrow, I thought perhaps you might be so disgusted with me you wouldn't want to have me in that intimate position but would rather bend me over the chair like a naughty boy, and smack me even harder - and so go on from day to day, making my position more and more humiliating and your chastisement ever more severe - progressing to the birch, perhaps, then the cane, and then - if I proved irredeemable - to the whip on my naked body trussed to the bedframe. Oh, but I promise it shall not come to that, dear master. You will not even need to spank me again tomorrow. I shall be a reformed character from this moment on. You'll see. I give you my solemn word."

What she actually gave me was the most beautiful smile - all the more so for its rarity. "Ah, well, then," I mumbled, beginning to rise again, "in that case, perhaps we'll overlook it just this once."

"However" - she thrust me back again, heavily - "to show you it is no cowardice on my part, but a genuine desire for reform, I insist on taking my punishment tonight." And she threw herself forward, belly down, upon my lap, settling her head and shoulders on the mattress of the bed, whose proximity she had judged to the inch. One hand snaked up behind her and began to tug impatiently at her dress.

I slapped it moderately hard. "You will leave that to me, if you please, miss."

She folded her arms beneath her head and lay contentedly upon them, a seraphic little smile beginning to play on her lips.

"Oh, G–," I sighed as I started to haul up her dress. "You could be such a charming, adorable little girl, and instead you go and misbehave like this. What are we going to do with you? Where will it all end?"

Beneath the dress was a frilly cotton petticoat. I began to raise that, too letting my hands caress the backs of her limbs as she had directed. "You used to be so good. So good. And now it's all dissolved in wickedness. Where do you get it, I wonder?"

"Please don't hurt me?" she begged, finding it hard to keep the warble of delight out of her tone.

Beneath the cotton petticoat was . . . another cotton petticoat! I began on that, too, with lots more caressing of her limbs. "Oh, please, dear master," she murmured. "I know you're only pretending to admire these revelations of my charms – to make my punishment more terrible when it comes. But if you desire me in that way, then take me. I'll do anything you want, only please don't hurt me."

Beneath that second cotton petticoat was a pair of long-legged drawers that descended below her knees in a cascade of frills and flounces. I began tugging at the drawstring around her waist, but she readjusted her position slightly, artlessly letting her legs part while she did so, thus revealing to me that the drawers were wide open through the fork.

To distract her, I reached my free left hand toward her charming young breasts which, though fully clothed, were hanging enticingly in the space between my lap and the edge of the bed. While she was getting over the shock of that I raised my other hand brought it down as hard as ever I could onto the thin material over her right posterior. And before the shock of that could register, I gave her another furious slap on the other cheek. Then another, and another, all on that same left cheek.

While she was still gasping at that I slipped my fingers down into the hot dark crevice whose two fine lips I could see, pouting and begging for such an invasion. Her juices were suddenly flowing like a troutbeck. "Oh . . . oh!" She was panting heavily from the shock of my spanking. One small tear ran down her cheek. But the smile on her lips was more seraphic than ever.

"What's this?" I asked angrily, as if I had found something to my annoyance down there. I withdrew my hand as if to explore from a different angle but instead gave her two more of the hardest slaps I could manage. She almost fainted in an ecstasy she disguised as a howl of pain.

My old rumpsplitter was himself pretty ecstatic by now, rearing up to my navel for a good look round and seeing nothing but the shrouds of my fancy dress. I had to tell him it would be some time yet before this little novelty would be ready for him; he understood, I think, but he wouldn't lie down.

Then, while my darling Miss G– was relishing her latest dole of pain, I slipped my hand into her fork again, this time with my knuckles moving and sliding among all her lips and folds. Thanks to Fleur's telling imagery I now became aware for the first time of the sticky little pops and crackles than an active hand can make as it swills among all that delicious juice. This time I got one knuckle against her flower, though I pretended I could not find it. "What's this?" I asked sternly. "Have you lost your virginity already? Who could have taken it? Name the scoundrel."

"No, no, it is there," she assured me, lifting her darling bottom and pouting more widely still.

"I feel nothing," I snapped. "I warn you, miss, if you have thrown away your delicate jewel I shall not spare you the most brutal and violent chastisement."

"But it is there! It is there, I promise," she cried desperately - and I almost fainted with my lust as she arched her back to the extreme limit, raising the two pale moons of her *derrière* and positively gaping at me with the lips of her upright smile. "I see it," I said gruffly - which was the truth. "No - stay still. Let me look and make sure."

"Feel it if you will," she whispered, reaching for my unseen fingers with that nether smile.

But my hand was already poised high overhead; its descent turned the last of her words into a squeal of terror that was surely heard all over the house - certainly if the little squeals of delight that I could hear coming *from* all over the house were any sort of guide.

Five or six times more my hand descended, each as hard as the last, if not harder. I don't know what it did to her bottom, it certainly left my hand hot and stinging with pain.

I intended to roger her at once after that, supposing that if I could introduce her to the more ordinary delights of our bodies so soon after her somewhat idiosyncratic pleasures, I might, in time, turn her into the most outstanding Daughter of Joy. But the moment I sported the Lad, he wilted! Yes, actually *wilted*. I look at the word on the page and still cannot believe it. It was not a general failing of my powers - as I proved only moments later with Fleur - but some specific refusal by the Lad for reasons of his own.

I can only assume he *has* his reasons and that they will one day become clear to me.

"Now profit from this lesson, G–," I said sternly, to hide my chagrin as I put the Lad back in his lair. "I hope I never have to chastise you like that again. But be warned - if I must, I shall. No flinching. And next time it will be on your bare posteriors."

I rose, spilling her onto the threadbare carpet, and made for the door. She struggled to her feet, raced after me, and threw herself about my knees, thanking me profusely and promising to be good for ever after.

Just as I was leaving she asked, "My *bare* posteriors?"

I turned and looked her directly in the eye. "That's a promise. You'd be a fool to imagine I don't mean it."

What an enigmatic smile she gave me in reply! I begin to nurture the strangest feelings about her. Is she a witch? Her eyes were tight-closed when I got out my girlometer to take the measure of her; she cannot have seen what happened – and yet her smile told me she knew of it. Indeed, it did more than tell, it assured me – even reassured me – that all was well. I almost felt as if I were part of her curriculum instead of her being part of mine. Well, we shall see about that, young lady! It is a situation no self-respecting Principal can tolerate.

For our lovers' tryst Fleur had chosen the Pompadour Room, with its opulent, gilded bed, its silken hangings, its elegant chaise longue and its wicked mirrors. It was unmistakably the room of a high-class courtesan.

"That was a splendid tale," I remarked. "I think they believed it, too."

"But it's true," she protested.

"Yes? Well, I have read something very like it in Maupassant."

She pouted. Women are without doubt the most wonderful things in all of Creation – and here was the cream of that cream. I was besotted with her already – her dark ringlets, the electric-blue eyes, and those delicate, finely modelled lips that not even Michelangelo could have captured. "I suppose," she said, "that if I had written of being taught to steal handkerchiefs – which is a trade of poor children all over France – you would accuse me of borrowing from Zola?"

I accepted the rebuke. "You are right, my dove. Pay no attention to me. I'm just jealous."

"Jealous?" The word startled her out of her pique.

"I'm jealous of all women," I explained. "You have – so naturally, so easily – you have the one thing I desire most in all the world to possess."

It knocked her off her high horse and brought the smile back to her lips. Before I realized what she was doing, she fell to her knees before me, threw up my toga or whatever the Beduwiyn call those long, loose robes, and took my girl-opener into her hands. She stared at it goggle-eyed and gave out one long-drawn gasp of surprise. Exciting as it is for a man to have his best friend fondled and stared at with such adoration by a pretty young girl, there are even more exciting things she might do with it after a minute or two. I was about to suggest a few when she opened wide her mouth, took the head of him inside, and sucked and gulped on me like a mad machine.

The sensation was like a sweet gimlet boring upward through my spine and out via my scalp. What is the secret of carnal pleasure? I have enjoyed these activities a thousand times before, and yet each repetition somehow retains a quality of uniqueness. Food is not like that. A bowl of strawberries and cream is a bowl of strawberries and cream. But each sweet hour of pleasure with a girl, even with the same girl and for the twentieth time, is still unique.

After only a few of those delicious sucks, from one of the liveliest – and certainly the loveliest – mouths that ever engulfed me, I had to pull out of her and take the firmest grip on my passion.

And on Fleur.

Virgin or not, there is an unrepeatable pleasure in undressing a willing young girl for the first time, especially one as voluptuous as Fleur, who hadn't a straight line or a flat surface anywhere about her. From her shoulders to half-way down her thighs her dress fitted her like a sheath; from her thighs to her ankles it billowed out in a profusion of silky frills and ruffles. I was desperate to get my hands down there, to tease it up toward her waist, to spread her thighs slowly wider, and feast my gaze on what their parting revealed.

But then her breasts were so delectable, too! They were the sort one sees far more often in lascivious drawings, alas, than in real life – full, beautifully rounded, and elevated to the most breathtaking degree. I have occasionally seen women endowed in that way – in shops, at the races, going about their ordinary business, and seeming quite unaware of the effect their charms are having on the unfortunate men around them. "What can their husbands or lovers be thinking of?" we ask ourselves in despair. "If we had free access to such adorable playthings, we should never rise from our beds." So I looked down on the tops of Fleur's breasts and rejoiced I was no longer in that miserable condemned cell of the unwilling voyeur. Her centre of bliss could wait – it would be the hotter, the sweeter, the wetter, for a little play at a higher *niveau*.

I told her she was one of the most exquisite women I had seen in many years and asked her if she would like to see that beauty through my eyes. Intrigued, of course, she said yes. I pulled a mirror to where it would give us both an alternative view of what I was about to do – which was to ease the material away from those perfect globes and air them. Oh, and she knew! She must have spent hours before her own looking glass, teasing and pleasuring herself up there. But more than that – she knew in her very blood how a man would look upon them, be inflamed by them, become her abject slave just for the touch and sight of them. To take them gently in my hands, to begin to fondle them and feel her nipples swell, was one of those rare *first* moments in life – one's first sip of Château d'Yquem, one's first pheasant downed on the wing, one's first silk sheets . . .

As soon as I held them she sighed and yielded herself up to me. From that moment on she seemed incapable of sitting – much less of standing – independently; her graceful arms were always about me, her curvaceously slender body always pressed to me. Her flesh was a furnace of longing, its every moment a provocation to my tormented friend below, which I feared would snap in two if it didn't find itself snug inside her soon. The hour or more of delighted foreplay I had envisaged from the moment I first set eyes on her dwindled to no more than ten minutes of that sweetest torment in the world. I did not even get my lips to her bud of joys. Every now and then she opened a drugged and drowsy eye to watch us in the mirror – until at last she lifted her gaze to me and begged, "Please – oh please . . ."

Her dress fell from her as I lifted her up and bore her to that enormous bed; I was already stark. I laid her on her back and put my hands to her thighs, but she rolled over at once onto her stomach and lifted her slim, firm bottom to me in a mute but undeniable plea. Her buttocks were like two pale, sand-coloured stones whose pressure in my groin was unbearably voluptuous as I lowered myself upon her. I could not see her face directly but, as the bedhead was a mirror, too, I could see her – indeed, both of us – there instead. My creamstick, with a life of his own by now, went straight to that wet, pulsating vestibule before the temple of paradise. I was surprised to notice her face screwed up, as if she were anticipating pain. I was so sure she was no virgin that it had not occurred to me to delay my entry there. Too late I felt her veil part before my importunate ramrod; too late I heard her cry of suffering – and then, hard on its heels, the balm of an incredulous laugh as I went to the very depths of that warm and giddy gullet.

Still only half believing her, I knelt up, grasping her below her hips and lifting her so as to fork her thighs wide against me. And there it was – as sweet a nuptial ring of crimson as any man could desire. The moment I saw it I was overwhelmed with tenderness and love for her – that she should have pretended to a voluptuary past she must have known this moment would unmask. I lay down then and let her take my full weight and coverage. She gasped with the pleasure of it and I rogered her all the way to a quick and easy climax with swift, deep, powerful strokes, well spaced apart and each one a surprise. She was a girl who responded to firmness – a firm embrace and firm, hard poking, deep into her holey of holeys. The very opposite of dear Abigail.

She was so inspiring, and so receptive to me, I was able to pleasure her twice more before we parted, tasting the delicious heat and the moist smoothness of her *corridor d'amour* from every possible angle – standing, sitting, kneeling, and back on the bed again, lying at full stretch. She was the best standing mistress I had ever known, with the glorious curve of her back as she leaned into me and the pert swelling of her bottom – all of which was a feast for my eyes in the tall mirrors all about us – and the way she lifted now one thigh, now the other, and draped it about me, making my stiff ruffian distend the walls of her *trou mignon* on each stroke. That seemed to give her exceptional pleasure, too, and turned our upright joy into one long disordered ecstasy for her.

"O milord!" she sighed when we had pleasured ourselves to exhaustion. "I will help you with these *innocentes du village sexuel,* I will be your . . .'ow you say – 'orse of Troye?"

"Will you indeed?"

"Yes. It is so much to teach them, but I 'elp, you see. When you wish *une petite poulette* to show them . . . tricks – ooh-la-la – you understand – I trace the path for them."

"Tu peut parler français, ma chère."

"No, I speaking only Eenglish now."

"In that case, my little deflowered Fleur, the blood that has glorified these sheets impels me to ask where have *you* learned such tricks?"

"Ah milord, il faut bien vivre, alors. Et qui vivra verra."

A girl must live, eh? And to live is to understand? What folly I had indulged – to hope for consistency and truth from a virgin French cocotte whose body was already a past mistress of male desires whose brunt she had never borne!

Apart from my precious Miss G–, there remained but one virgin among my darling pupils: Jonquil. And if true virginity be a state of maiden-*mind* rather than of maiden-*head,* I suspected she would remain in that unhappy condition even if I did nothing but roger her "from arseholes to breakfast time", as a Guardsman I used to enjoy once put it.

I found her in the library, reading *Lady Pokingham* –

or They All Do It. The moment she saw me she snapped the book shut like a guilty schoolgirl and began to giggle.

"Come on," I said.

She trotted to me like an obedient little spaniel. I took her up to the nursery and stripped her without finesse; there would have been no point in doing otherwise for she continued to giggle every time I touched her, and, simultaneously, she performed a peculiar movement I can only describe as trying to hide inside herself. It was indeed strange. She had a body absolutely made for sexual congress; it is hard for a man, looking at such perfection and feeling himself roused almost beyond his control, to believe that no corresponding lust is burning inside that object of his longing. Jonquil, I feel sure, had never entertained a sexual thought in her life, never fingered her own privities, never felt that sweet rapture of having her breasts fondled or her nipples sucked and caressed. It was as if we were back in the nursery playing doctors and nurses. Everything was a giggle.

I made her kneel on all fours in that outsize cradle, like a dog, with her *derrière* up in the air and her full, pale breasts hanging free. Then I lay beneath her in what would eventually be *soixante-neuf*, except that my lips were at present level with her breasts, which I now eased down into my mouth. She giggled again, but not for long. I sucked hard at her nipples, slowly opening my teeth so that her flesh would be drawn inward in a contact that bordered on pain. She gave out a gasp, and giggled no more. I did it again, more gently. And then again, several times, until her breathing became heavier. There was at last a satisfactorily dreamy look in her eyes.

I laid her on her back and, straddling her, went again at her breasts, this time with my fingers and fingernails. She closed her eyes and began to shake her head from side to side, saying, "Oh!" and "Ah!" as if she could not believe the sensations now arising spontaneously inside her. I went down on her then, tasting the lovely tangy nectar of an ash-blonde cranny. She had one of the most baroque *concons* I had ever seen - one seething mass of fleshy whorls and convolutions, a spaghetti of folds and tucks with a pleasure-button like a damask rose. There I feasted to my heart's - and tongue's - content. She no longer knew nor cared what I was doing. She had vanished into that private world of her own senses, where she wandered in awe at the joys which had been hiding within her, unsuspected all these years.

She swelled to within a hairsbreadth of a climax, but her body - and, I suspect, her emotions, too - knew not how to make that final leap. I did all I could to help her but to no avail. She threshed around, shaking her head wildly, gasping, choking, shivering . . . she was racked and tormented by a pleasure just short of that final, shattering eruption. At last, tearing off my clothing, I resolved to poke her without delay. She was so wet I had little difficulty getting the tip of my rascal against her maiden portal, which yielded to my third importunate knock. "See!" I said, withdrawing my merry-maker to show her his blush of triumph.

She stared at him a while and then fell back on the pillow. I thought she had surely fainted, but the smile on her lips was one of joy. I moved all the way into her then. Her *trou* was as baroque as everything else down there. I remember swimming under water once and being so roused by the sinuous movement of the seaweed in the ebb and flow of the tide that I took out my rantallion and tried to roger a bunch of it; Jonquil's inner haven was like that - only warm.

It was still the same story, though. I could bring her within moments to the very brim of her climax, but she could not take that final step. I turned her over and enjoyed her from behind, working simultaneously on that generous rosebud and her firm young nipples. The same thing happened. When, after several other positions, it became clear that all my skill was simply not enough to work that ancient miracle, I decided to forgo my own climax, too - it would have seemed a kind of boasting to proceed to that point without her. So I began the gentle process of winding her - and myself - down again. For the final quarter of an hour we just lay side by side, kissing and caressing one another. Not a giggle out of her - so that was a good start, I felt.

She said it had been beautiful. I told her how beautiful *she* was and gave no hint that we had both failed to reach the mountain top. One day I shall find the trick of it - and then she will astonish herself. I now feel very warm toward my dear little Jonquil.

> "A well brought up young female of good background is unlikely ever spontaneously to acquire an interest in such earthy topics; therefore her curiosity, however lively it may be in other, healthier directions, will never be aroused, and she will live out her life in the sweet bliss of the domestic round, doing her little charities, attending her minor chores, never once troubled by those rages that so disfigure the inner lives of men."

> "It is a delusion under which many a previously incontinent man suffers to suppose that in newly married life he will be required to treat his wife as he used to treat his mistresses. It is not so in

the case of any modest English woman. He need not fear that his wife will require the excitement, or in any respect imitate the ways of the courtezan."

I shall not embarrass the authors of these pompous asininities by naming them here; it is enough to their shame and ours that they are accounted among the foremost thinkers of our time on the delicate subject of female sexuality. Worse still, most men now living would agree with them.

To the average male in this, the first decade of the twentieth century, females are divisible into two groups. The well-bred, well-brought-up young women are untouchable vestals, creatures to be worshipped, venerated, pampered – eventually, one supposes, married. The rest were made by a kindly Creator for chaps like me – that is, above ninety-nine percent of all men (for chastity is as dead as the dodo now).

And why not, indeed? For is it not a brilliant arrangement? Our wives sit happily at home, as naturally chaste as Penelope, singing to our children in the nursery and planning little surprises for our comfort and delight. And we, in return, duly worship them for it. And when those other, sinful urges overwhelm us, as they are apt to do once or twice a day, we spare our delectable, contented angels and find some common sewer for our ejaculations.

I have argued against such shallow beliefs all my life, not from any intellectual standpoint but from the profoundest conviction that they deprive both men and women of their greatest joy. In this morning's lessons with my five sweet nymphs – plus Miss G – I tried to make this clear. Mind you, I do not wish them to become forward young hussies. God forbid! But I wish them to cultivate that open and honest hedonism that will neither fly from pleasure nor, what is worse, enjoy it as something dirty and shameful – wallowing, as it were, in what should be pleasant and wholesome.

Miss G–, of course, as part of her constant campaign to force me to expel her, immediately produced some "research" from the library. She has been studying, she *says,* the Colonel's collection of erotic texts from the Orient; she claims it was at my suggestion, though it is no such thing. All I said was that I believe the Orientals had a healthier attitude to sexual matters than we of the Occident, with our Judeo-Christian idiocy on the subject. But does that mean we have to adopt *everything* they do, lock, stock, and barrel?

Anyway, this is what she produced; she calls it a "pot-pourri" of oriental wisdom!

The Love-Ecstasy of the Oriental Maiden
by Miss G–

The Wisdom of the Orient in venereal matters runs ancient and deep. They know that the man is the audacious leader in all matters of love. He is the tireless hunter, the ardent wooer, the indefatigable prize-taker, whereas the female is passive and silent, withdrawn into her modesty, waiting to be aroused and taken. It is so through every stage of their courtship.

When their eyes first meet, his burn with the spark of his passion, which is ever swift to kindle; she looks away and avoids her lord's gaze. Perhaps already she feels the petty shivering of her desire, yet she would rather die than reveal it. Later, when her lord seeks her out to make the most passionate declarations of his love, she will watch him steadily with those cool, almond eyes until he stammers himself silent. Even if she is the merest courtezan, who can be bought for a few idly tossed coins, she will do these things, for it is the natural way with every Oriental maid.

When her lord has entreated her for the hundredth time to sing or dance for him she will at last consent. And now she will show the deep division of her nature to the utmost. Her song will be full of suggestive vibrations; her voice will flutter, her lips tremble. Her dance will be so lascivious you would swear every bone in her spine had turned to jelly; yet not the smallest glimpse of her private charms will she reveal. Notwithstanding that, her lord will sit there transfixed, convinced he is seeing all. Throughout her performance her gaze is withdrawn and no smile disturbs her lips. She communes, as it were, with some inner pool of bliss – which will not be completed until her lord joins her there.

And this is hardest for our Occidental minds to grasp. Her bliss is all inward, all buried, all penned up, inside her. She needs her lover but she does not go to him; he must come to her. Her lord brings no happiness to her; only the discovery of it. It is not something that passes from him to her when their bodies are joined. It is there within her all along; but without him she cannot find it. She is the flower; he the sun.

And nowhere is the difference between Orient and Occident more plain than in the act of congress itself, the rituals for which may commence for the woman hours or even days before her lover arrives. She must bathe, pluck her hair, annoint her body with sweet-smelling oils, place subtle perfumes in every crevice. Occidental commentators have assumed that all these preparations are intended to heighten the pleasure of the lord – which, naturally, they do. But that is not their purpose. For during those long hours of tender ministration the Maid is forced to concentrate upon the marvels and mysteries of her own body. It is a ritual to focus all her thoughts and feelings inward, to those central mysteries of her sex. The deeper she goes, the more she becomes aware how precious she is, how special her body, how wondrous all its secret places. By the time her lord appears, she is a smouldering volcano of desire, ready to erupt.

He, too, has been considerate in his preparations, abstaining from venery until he is undermined and hollowed out with his longing, and washing and annointing his every part. And it is now that we see the greatest difference of all. For that moment he touches her she passes, as it were, into a light trance. She does not stamp and whinny like a mare at stand, as is the way with the bolder Occidental woman - indeed, it is almost as if she has lost the power of independent volition. Here is Sula-ma'Haiyia, Queen of Hadhraphut in the Fourth Century AD, describing the first of her four nuptial nights:

"When my lord the King had disrobed me and satisfied his eyes, he led my fingers to his broach, which, when I eased its pin, let slip his raiment and revealed his manhood in pride. He was still seated upon his golden stool and now he caused me to approach him, parting my thighs over his until our bodies touched and his lingam nuzzled at my arbour of heaven. Then he pulled me down, not so that he went inside but so that his nuzzling there became intense. And there he began to caress my flesh as he might annoint it, both with his fingers and his lips.

"When he took my breasts between his teeth, it gave me such pleasure I believed I should pass out. Well schooled as I was, I struggled to keep all sign of it from my features. But it was hard, since all these joys, though oft described and accidentally witnessed as I have already told, were novel to my flesh and senses. I wrestled my pleasure, using some strange inward hands that pinioned it within me and forced it deeper and yet deeper in its urgency to move. But I could not help a spasm that shook my eyes and lids, making me drowsy with desire. My lord saw it and, smiling at my inexperience, relaxed his provocation of my longing. He was well pleased to have startled me into such a revelation; yet he would not have welcomed my prolonging such a shameful exhibition.

"Later, when he laid me down among silken cushions, and we grazed upon each others' bodies as the wild deer graze the plains, he helped me discover the well of my pleasure more precisely. Now I had a focus for each new sensation. Now I could begin to weave that golden thread which, in the finest of women, stretches from the crown of her scalp to the soles of her feet; whose vibrations are tuned by her lord's every move; whose harmonies are the climax of her joys at being so used.

"When he could no longer confine his rapture to my skin but must know my flesh as well, he caused me to kneel over his golden stool, my thighs well parted, while he knelt behind me and slowly annointed the tip of his lingam, up and down in my furrow of joys. I could not help giving out one deep sigh of contentment at that restless touch – nor a second when I felt his belly against my haunches and the sudden pressure of him in my innermost quarters. Again, I think these small lapses of mine pleased him, though he did nothing to show his approval.

"After that I struggled with all my might to contain my delirium, to increase its power and plant it deeper, ever deeper, within. I know not how long we continued nor how many positions my lord desired me to adopt and so multiplied my pleasure in his trespass, for I soon entered a most curious state of ecstasy. It was like a trance in its outward stillness, yet like a rage, a fever, a drunkenness within. It seized up every particle of my flesh, every bone and sinew, and made it a hopeless, passionate slave to that quivering well of delights in the depths of my belly . . ."

And so on. Her description of what we Occidentals call the four-legged frolic or the matrimonial polka (or worse) contains no further reference to any physical action. There is no "he fondled my breasts . . . caressed my peachlike bottom . . ." and so on – none of the gems that strew out erotic literature like good marl upon a barren moor, encumbering what it cannot enrich. And yet I would challenge any European writer of such titillations to match her description of a woman's sexual initiation for sheer erotic power.

So whereas our dear, sweet Horny would encourage us to come out of that shell of modesty and indifference in which we have all been reared, I commend to you, my dear sisters, the very opposing course. Our feminine pleasures are *not* to be found in aping young hoydens, shrieking and gasping at every prod of his dear Old Lad. We shall do far better to take the Oriental path to our innermost happiness.

She closed her notebook and smiled sweetly all round. The others looked at me in some trepidation, expecting me, no doubt, to explode in wrath at this most direct challenge yet to my "authority" as their teacher.

"Why not?" I said simply. "If it works, why not? Give it a try."

Miss G– rose and stalked from the room in high dudgeon. She is so young, so lovely in her youthfulness, in the very naïveté of her passions, I confess I almost *love* her.

It was an obscure kind of victory for me and I felt I ought to consolidate it in some way. My first impulse was to follow her to her room and drive home my point in the most obvious and appropriate way. But one brief, internal consultation with the Lad was enough to warn me off; not the smallest flicker of interest could I detect down there.

Why? I keep asking myself. And I grow almost fearful to know.

Was anything ever more fickle than woman? I declare, my faith in them is shattered. Having framed myself - mind, body, and spirit - to try out this new Oriental wheeze of Miss G–'s, what happens? Why, the very opposite, of course. I should have forbidden it utterly; then we'd have had five of the most passive, docile maidens who ever shivered their way through a settlement in tail.

As it is, however, they have taken the hoyden's course. Our leading authorities on the subject of female sexuality (or lack of same) should see my scholars now. When it comes to matters of lewdness and depravity, of insatiability, of indecent invention, of coarse humour, of indelicate ingenuity . . . in short, of every branch of sexual prowess where we men have thought the laurels were ours, a delicate, well-bred angel will leave us at the post; she will beat us hands down, prick down, head down.

You ask for proof? Come visit my academy of well-brought-up young ladies, at any hour of the day or night, and you shall find proof. I cannot write of it now, though I shall try anon. I am too shaken by the things I have heard and seen.

Yet I will say this: Were I dictator of the world, I should enforce upon pain of death an universal belief in the idiotic teachings I have already quoted. They are damnable lies but it would be better by far for society that all should believe them than that the truth were known. For if women - that half whom we think of as angels, *and who think of themselves as angels,* too – if they were ever to learn the truth about themselves as my young "angels" here are doing, we men should know neither peace of body when we are with them nor peace of mind when we are not. They would turn us into sexual performers at the crack of their whim. Or the whim of their crack.

The fact is that women are by nature neither angels nor whores – nor anything else – *by nature*. They are, as it were, a blank slate upon which, by some mysterious *collective* process, they write a recipe of each other's souls. I feel there must exist somewhere a grisly female *supra*mind, a vast collective Female Will composed of millions of individual female wills, which decrees what they shall be at any particular time in history or place in the world. The "scandalous" behaviour of our great grandmothers in the days of the Regency was imposed on individual women by the collective, abstract Woman of that time – the idealized picture every woman pins up in the mirror of her soul. For most of the late and unlamented century quite the opposite Ideal Woman was pinned up there; yet see how our females have conformed! And it is the same with Miss G–'s passive Orientals, too; they have a collective mind to be as they are, and so they all conform.

That, indeed, is the true nature of Woman – to conform to the current ideal. I do not mean mere slavery to fashion; it goes far deeper than that. Their fashion-slavery is but a trivial consequence of that profound urge to conform.

The question still remains: What has happened here in my jolly little Academy to change them? What has turned six demure young virgins into these monsters of depravity and lust? It would be both flattering and tempting (since none can contradict me) to say that my old friend, my one-eyed spermspouter, has done the magic. But it is not so. I am as bemused and horrified as any would be who heard and saw what I have lately seen.

I dread to advance what I believe the true reason, and yet I must. It is this: The lechery, the pleasure-seeking soul, the lust that I have seen revealed *is* the blank slate of Woman's soul. This female monster, this mænad, this bacchante of carnal appetite *is* your unreconstructed woman. She sits there at the core of every nun, every vestal, Everyman's revered mother, Everyman's honoured sister. She is the primeval, prime-evil Eve – the first and greatest temptress.

What other explanation is there? All I have done is to remove them from the censorious vigilance of the outside world. The rest has followed as night the day. Pandora's box, I now understand, was her own innermost nature – and here I have opened it six times over!

I saw it happen before my very eyes, this transformation. I observed how they read their way through my erotic library, how they tried out little fantasies in their essays to be read out in class – each egging on the other to go one small but daring step further than last time. And before any of us realized what was happening, they were in headlong flight from Angel to Eve.

And yet I know that if they returned to the world outside, the old Ideal would snap back into place in an instant; while they are here, however, a more ancient Woman-power rules. The only homage they pay to Darling House-Angel is that they disguise their more degraded fantasies as "dreams." Indeed, *My Dream* is the commonest essay they submit; it invariably heads a farrago of filth that would bring a blush to the cheek of a Bankside tart.

One sample will suffice. It is from Abigail but any of them could have written it. It is also a kind of semi-conscious refutation of Miss G–'s Oriental thesis:

ABIGAIL: In another incarnation I was Empress of a great Oriental country. Visiting ambassadors had to present their credentials to me in the liveliest fashion. [Here is an obscene drawing of a man in a turban holding suggestively a yard-long roll of paper with two huge seals dangling below it.] Once seven of them presented at once and my one hole, even after such energetic traffic could accommodate but two, so one must make do with my bumhole, another my mouth, two more my hands, and the last must make his own tunnel between my ample dairies. Ah, Seven! Dear Seven! Sweet Seven! No wonder you are called the Mystic, Magic Number . . .

And so on. This is Abigail! Dear, sweet, adorable, shy little Abigail! Where will it end? (In fact, now that I remember it, that particular essay ended in an argument, which was only resolved when my servant Nimrod and I, plus five girls wearing rubber dildoes, attempted to prove that it was, indeed, possible – though desperately uncomfortable and nothing like as much fun as a nice gentle poke by one man on a hearthrug before the fire.)

This misrule has extended even into the sweetest of our lessons, when I, their teacher, take them aside to this room or that and coach them individually in the arts of love. No sooner are we tasting the joys that make such lessons so rewarding for us both than in burst the rest, flushed and excited with private exercises of their own, demanding "their share" and joining in without a by-your-leave. Orderly instruction becomes impossible in such conditions; we simply abandon all idea of amatory progress and wallow in the most debased voluptuousness.

Miss G– alone stands apart – or, rather, stood apart until yesterday. Then she adopted a new trick.

When I asked her to read out her latest essay, this is what we heard:

Miss G–'s unspoken question

There was once a certain nobleman who caused a chamber to be built within his house, and this chamber was intended exclusively for his pleasure with women And there her caused to be led, day by day, a succession of females of every degree. High-born, low-born, or of a middling rank, they were all one to him, for in his carnal dispensation no greater democrat ever breathed. And his method of pleasure was thus.

His manservant would carry in a succession of little notes, instructing the woman how she was to undress, which of her charms she was to display, and by what means. Meanwhile he stood without and ogled her through the keyhole. By and by, as his passions overpowered him, he would burst into the room, throw his paramoor upon the bed, and ravish her mightily. And then he would pay her – for that particular debt was more sensitive to him than honour itself and it was his proudest boast that he never sent away an unrewarded wench.

And when he had enjoyed nine hundred and ninety-nine women after this strange fashion, his manservant said to him, "Oh, master, you have enjoyed so many women. Tomorrow it will be a thousand. You must know and understand womankind better than any man living!"

"Why, I suppose I do," he replied, preening himself in the glass, "Indeed I do."

And when the nine hundred and ninety-nine women came to hear of this reply (and the thousandth, too, whom he enjoyed that day), they laughed until they almost split their sides.

* * *

I considered this an utterly pointless tale and deliberate waste of our precious time. But for some reason the other girls pretended to see a profound truth in it, which, for the first time, aroused me to anger.

"Leave the class," I snapped at her. "Go to your room."

"Not now!" she said; and I saw in her eyes that bizzare look which is both terror and joy.

In fact, it had not been my intention to chastise her then. It was our habit to punish her after supper each evening, and I had supposed the inevitability of that hour – watching the minute hand drag its way round the clock – was part of her strange pleasure. Now I saw that the idea of a sudden Nemesis, out of the blue, had its own piquancy for her, too.

"Yes," I snarled, acting it up a bit, for curiosity was, as always with Miss G–, pushing aside my annoyance. "Now! And this will be no play session, miss. You have gone too far. Now I shall show you who is master here."

"Oh, please!" She flung herself prostrate at my feet, clinging to my ankles. "I take it all back. I didn't mean a word of it. I was joking."

I could see that his absurd little scene was having an undesirable effect on my other girls. Their eyes were gleaming with excitement; their lips hung open in a most particular and unmistakable delight.

In a new rage I seized up the wretched Miss G– by her hair and delivered a stinging slap to her face. She burst into tears and fled, with me hard on her heels – and five young minxes hard on mine.

But I got there, to G–'s garret, just in time to bolt the door in their faces. Uttering loud cries of disappointment they fled.

"Now, miss," I said menacingly, throwing off my

jacket and rolling up my sleeve with slow deliberation.

She went through all the usual antics – that strange mixture of pleas for me to show mercy when all the time she was struggling out of her clothes as fast as ever she could. We had already progressed beyond the friendly little spanks across my knee; now she bent over the back of a chair and grabbed its front legs immediately below the seat, just like anyone on the block at Eton.

This time, however, *I* went further. I pulled the silken cord from her dressing gown, which hung behind the door, and knelt before the chair to bind her to it at her wrists. As I did so, I caught that lovely, wild, musky tang of the redhead off her skin, saw her two plump young breasts dangling there in the most enticing way, and it almost broke my heart. If only she could find *true* pleasure, I thought – in the normal way – what a superb lover she would be! And then I caught that mad gleam of fearful ecstasy in her eye . . .

Did she see the fear unalloyed in mine? I first indulged this whim of hers for pain out of curiosity – both about myself and her. Never in my life did I imagine it would take such a hold on me as well. I feel I stand now, in relation to this new form of sex as I once stood to its more natural embodiment in my fantasies with young Becky, the gardener's daughter. I sense that a pleasure, as yet unknown, awaits me there – sexual, of course, but something else beside. When I see G–'s glorious young form bent shivering over that chair, with her little pink lips and her pale auburn bush peeping out of that nook below her bum, when I see the moons of her *derrière,* trembling and pale as they anticipate the fall of my hand, I know that a pleasure awaits my discovery as profound as any I have yet experienced.

And yet I fear it as I never feared those earlier joys,

for who knows where it might lead – to what dark corners of my soul, to what monsters of unpublished lust that lurk within me.

Already I was in the grip of some new frenzy – else I would have known that I had taken off one of my slippers and held it now in my hand. Yet I did not know it till I raised it over my head and brought it down on her slim, inviting bottom with every ounce of my strength. Her shriek of pain touched off a twittering chorus of frustrated excitement beyond the door. A red mist of anger rose before my eyes. All the fury of these past days – watching the control of my girls slip from my grasp – and knowing that Miss G– was at the heart of it – all that now filled me with a lust for revenge.

Again I flailed at her with my slipper – a stout leather one that was a shoe in all but weight and flexibility. What was the nature of such intense yet short-lived pain? I wondered. Did the savaged flesh proclaim, "Every corpuscle for itself!"? Did the unharmed inches offer up prayers of thanks, "Lord I praise you that I am not as those wretches over there?" Did the body turn to war upon itself? Ask any general – the most enjoyable war of all for a military man is a civil war. Has the body long ago discovered that secret, too? And is that the chief attraction of this form of sex?

Again and again I wielded the slipper, determined to leave no flesh that might offer up such prayers. Miss G– screamed in earnest and, hobbled as she was, attempted to crab-walk the chair away from me. But I leaped before her and, thrusting her head down between my thighs clamped her tight and laid it on again with gusto.

During this commotion I must have failed to notice that the minxes outside were battering down the door with a bench taken from the schoolroom. No sooner had I got Miss G–'s head well clamped than the lock splintered and in they all tumbled.

But my surprises did not end there. I recovered from the immediate shock of their intrusion only to hear them bleating out in chorus, "Me, too! Me, too . . .!"

"Don't imagine I wouldn't," I roared.

With squeals of joy they threw me several light switches of peeled and oiled willow – and started to peel themselves. Abigail and Eve were the first to stand naked – but not for long. They dragged the bench across to beside the bed and flung themselves down with their tummies on the seat, their lovely breasts hanging free in the space between, and their heads cradled on their folder arms upon the bed. The others swiftly joined them – including, I now saw, Miss G–, whom one of them must have untied.

They giggled and squirmed and wriggled until all their bottoms were touching and not so much as a playing card could have been squeezed between any two of them. And I have to confess, though I do so with shame, that the sight of those six wriggling young bottoms, so soft against the hardness of the bench, and twelve bare breasts (I could not see more than two or three, of course, but my mind's eye fleshed out the rest) hanging free, and six delightful young faces, all with their eyes closed, smiling dreamily, awaiting the fall of the cane, and the tangle of pretty locks spilling down over those curvaceous backs, and the little wisps of girlish moss peeping out from the cleft of their thighs . . . I have to confess it was the most powerfully erotic thing I ever saw.

I confess, too, that I came right off the moment the willow bit into that long pale nimbus of quivering flesh. Not a great spermspouting climax but a palpitating, thready sort of thrill that oozed a clean, clear milt out of old One-Eye and left the shaft of him gleaming and slippery. I lost count of the cuts I gave them but my trousers were soused with my own juice by the time I finished. I cannot say it was the most joyous ecstasy ever; in fact, I cannot call it an ecstasy in that sense at all. But the peace that followed it, the relief – I would even call it *release* – was as profound as any I had ever known.

I looked down at them, my six eager pupils. There were no smiles now. They were all shivering uncontrollably with the shock. Jonquil was weeping quietly. Fleur was gasping as it she had run a mile. The rest, their eyes still closed, had a faraway expression I could not even begin to plumb.

I looked down at the Lad, still rearing to go. At last, I thought, this was my chance to roger Miss G– into submission – the right and proper way between a man and a woman. I knelt behind my exhausted darlings and gave them a few tender pokes each, one by one, down the line. Eve, with her tight, tender little hole. Wilhelmina, receptive and warm. Fleur, voluptuous and knowing. Abigail, gluttonous and muscular. Jonquil, baroque and engulfing. And Miss G– . . .

But what Miss G– was like I cannot say. The Lad flinched and shrivelled even in those few inches that separated her from darling Jonquil. I watched in utter amazement as he vanished. It put me in mind of something once told me by Jenny – my father's present on my seventeenth birthday. One of her lovers found satisfaction only in being humiliated. He would call her "mistress" and crawl around on his belly, kissing her feet and asking her to hurt him. In the end he would roger her in the usual way but she had to keep telling him how useless he was at it. "I once tried a little test of him," she told me. "In between saying how disgusting and awful he was I'd slip in bits of encouragement – saying, 'Ooh! That's better! . . . Yes, yes! I'm enjoying that!' and so on. And d'you know, I could feel his dick shrivelling inside me. Then I'd have to shout at him and tell him he was even more useless than before – and then it would leap up again, stiff as a ramrod, ready for more.'' She'd grown so skilled at it, in fact, that she could make his pego as stiff or as limp as she wanted.

Curious now, I moved back to my sweet Jonquil, who was reaching her bottom toward me, begging for more with her downy young lips. The Lad leaped at her like a slipped greyhound. She wriggled and squeezed deliciously as he nosed into the old haven. I gave her a few deep, hard thrusts, just to confirm the Lad in his recovered status, and then, quick as a flash, whipped him out and leaped upon Miss G–. If I'd got him in at once, on that first stab, I'd have done it. But in my excitement I missed, so that his upper half slid harmlessly down her furrow and emerged at her mons, wearing the full length of her sex like a fur mantle. Less than a second later he fell from that embrace and hung as soft as a hazel catkin.

Miss G– opened her eyes – or the left one, which was all I could see – and smiled a most knowing smile. A million miles away the gong rang for luncheon.

What have I started? Every time I try to reassure myself that matters cannot possibly get any worse, they get worse. I should have studied the classics harder at school. All those tales about Pandora's box and the fellow who flew too close to the sun, they may all be symbolic – I mean, no man ever flew with a contraption of feathers and beeswax – but there's a horrible truth at the heart of them, those old legends.

A real warning for people like me who try to go against Nature.

For what *is* the nature of woman, eh? I am the first to admit they are the most complicated, maddening, adorable creatures one could possibly imagine – but only when left in the state Nature intended, which is a state of happy ignorance. A woman is a collocation of warm, responsive, curvaceous flesh arranged around a sensual hole; and somewhere in that vicinity, hidden among the trembling folds of that captivating haven, is a capacity for ecstasy that can almost kill her if only the right man is there to awaken it. And there's the point, you see – the *right* man. For if the wrong man assays the same performance, her indifference may shrivel into actual slumber – indeed it is so, for many's the girl has told me.

A woman, then, is very like a superb musical instrument, a grand piano, let us say. And what happens to a grand piano when its virtuoso is away? Why, nothing! There it stands in its domestic niche, silent, beautiful, unmoved, and unmoving. Stray notes from the world about it (which we may liken to stray memories of sexual pleasure) may stir faint harmonic resonances within its strings; but soon they fade and die. Incompetent fingers may conjure "My Old Man" and others discords from its innards; but the piano itself is quite unable to guide and correct them. Only when the maestro returns and cajoles it with his magic touch is it once again capable of those grand sonorities, those sublime cadences, those rapturous paeans of joy for which it was truly intended.

Fool that I am, I have often and often chafed at this niggardly arrangement. Women whom I have helped discover the most ravishing spasms of which their flesh is capable have nonetheless to be wooed and wheedled and whined into each and every subsequent excursion upon that ocean of bliss. Yet it is *their* ocean! They carry it within them, deep in their own marrow, ready to pour its libations to their orgasmic flesh – compared with which the brief, spermspouting leap of a man's five inches is, indeed, but "My Old Man" to all of Handel. I confess it: Part of my eternal obsession with women in that state of heavenly euphoria is the hope that one day I will know its mysteries, too. One day, whatever mind-blockage now prevents me from experiencing their monstrous, all-engulfing pleasure as if it were my own will at last yield – and then I will *know* the ultimate secret of all things.

Put like that, of course, it is absurd. The maestro might as well desire to *become* his own piano. Yet from the moment I feel my body naked against that of an ardent young woman, the absurdity of my quest vanishes. As the warmth of that sweetest space in the universe engulfs my beating lance of love, the old ambitions kindle once more. And when she starts to drown in those darling moans and shudderings, when all the air in the world is still not enough to feed those fires that rage within, when her sweat and honey flow over me in haemorrhage, then indeed I feel I stand but a whisker from victory.

The tragedy is that she who *knows* – so easily, so intimately – what I so desperately wish to learn can then rise, wash herself, hum an inconsequential tune, pat a stray lock of hair, return to our bed, give a little yawn, and say, "Hug me gently till I nod off, there's a pet." And what, my dearest, did you think of the Great God Pan? "Oh" – another little yawn – "he was very nice."

I have chafed, I say, at this unfairness; but no more! Take note, gentle reader: I, Lord Hornington, do hereby avow and affirm that the state of joyful semi-oblivion in which women exist between their frenzies of semi-oblivious joy is the only true, safe, and natural state for that entire sex.

I have often ranted at the ignorance in which we rear our tender flowers. Jove, I have said, it is as if a lion tamer were to rear his children to the trade without ever telling them that lions can eat people. No more! I hereby further swear that, if I survive these dreadful days, I shall go into parliament and there make it my life's work to revive the ancient punishment of Pressing to Death, followed by Hanging, Drawing, and Quartering for any person who, in any way whatsoever, seeks to enlighten the female race as to what unbounded delights lie instinctual in their flesh.

For here is the other universal humour of the holey tribe: What *one* does, *all* must do. The same is true of men, to be sure – yet in precisely the opposite sense. If you see a gang of men going down the street, the chances are they are bent on breaking the law, defying convention, kicking against society's ways. But a gang of women? Never – unless it be to tar and feather one of their sisters for *flouting* the conventions of society in some spectacular and flagrant manner! Ah yes, *then* you might assemble such a gang of females.

However, it is one thing to know that these sexual distinctions exist; it is quite another to be at their mercy. If I had only limited myself to Eve and Wilhelmina, what a happy little sodality of sensual love we should now enjoy. But no, I saw Fleur's voluptuous ripeness and must possess it; I smelled Abigail's redhead fragrance and must drown myself in it; I encountered Jonquil's girlish innocence and must turn it to grateful experience; and I sensed in the Miss G– some haunting promise whose siren enticement I could not deny. And because I must, must,

must have all of these, I am now drowning in the flood tide of their erotic liberation.

It is not that I wilt and fail before their combined onslaught. If only I might! How I pray for that blissful impotence! If one of my ravening little vixens were to press her ardent sex to mine, and all her pleas and whimpers, all her delightful writhings, still left my one-eyed friend as limp as lettuce, I would sacrifice all I had to that Antipriapus. But no; my release is not to be so easy. They know they need but flash me a glimpse of those sequestered delights and he will throb and swell. Even when I lie in exhausted slumber, and my spouter has spent till he aches, they will slip between the sheets and back their cool, pneumatic *derrières* into my groin and I wake to find him hot and rampant in his agony, rodding away as if Death stood patiently by.

And what *one* wants, *all* must have. They read these books, you see. (That's another thing. When I'm in parliament, anyone who permits erotic literature to fall into the hands of decent young women will be boiled in oil.) Anyway, they read these books – which any sensible man knows are only for titillation and not at all to be taken seriously – and they want to try out every little detail in reality. I write these words now in the throes of an exhaustion I almost wish were terminal (while they, thank Venus, are half-way through Sappho and the thousand and one nights of Lesbos – which they will doubtless curtail to three or four and be on my back once more, and front, and side, and top, and bottom . . . oh, my bottom!) . . . where was I? Yes – terminal exhaustion. So I cannot recall each and every stage, even if I wished to. But this was something of the way of it:

They began shortly after that class spanking, which had been prompted by Miss G–. (She, by the by, remains an enigma. She is still the lewdest and most forward of them all – and yet she remains a virgin! She ploughs her own lonely furrow toward her own lonely enlightenment. I watch with fascination. In a curious way, although I have not yet enjoyed her, and wonder if I ever shall, I feel I am more bound up with her destiny than with any of the others, though I know by now every pore of their hateful, delicious, tyrannical, yielding, insatiable young bodies.) Well, shortly after the class spanking, as I say, Abigail took it into her head to wonder what it was like for a girl to be poked, as brusquely and unfeelingly as possible, in circumstances very far from voluptuous – as it might be, down in the cellar on a dusty brick floor.

The answer was: "Not at all pleasant." Lord what a surprise! So, fortunately, they only tried it once. At least – and here's where my troubles begin – they only tried it once, *each*; I, therefore, had to endure it five times: on the cellar floor, in the scullery among congealed grease and soap scum, in the potting shed, on a heap of very sharp beech leaves left over from last autumn, and in the stifling heat and bat-guano reek of one of the lofts.

And yet, though they all declared it hateful, somehow the idea of being degraded or roughly used during the four-legged frolic had taken their fancy; and nothing would satisfy them till they had explored it to the bitter end. It was Jonquil who first asked me to oblige her deeper in this way. She begged me to command her, not angrily but unfeelingly, to bend over a chair, whereupon I was to tie her at the ankles and wrists so that she could not rise. And then I was to stand behind her and poke her as hard as I could. Each swift and powerful thrust was to contrast with the most gentle and loving of withdrawals. Slowly and tenderly I was to pull right out of her until the angry red tip of my Lad was beating with my racing heart, up and down between the downy folds of her gleaming cunny. And then I was to hammer into her again as hard and fast as I could.

I have to admit that I was at that stage a most willing volunteer to gratify these (as I thought) delightful fancies. To behave toward a woman in that manner was as novel to me as it seemed thrilling to her. All my life I had considered sexual pleasure to be a cooperative act between two equal partners, who were, so to speak, on the same emotional side. The idea of ordering a woman about and behaving as if her pleasure were of no consequence to me was utterly alien to my nature and my most cherished beliefs. And yet, when the woman herself demanded it, I cannot deny I found a certain perverse pleasure in gratifying the whim; in the same spirit one might sample Chinese cuisine or Transylvanian wine. But when all five of them clamoured for me to mistreat them in this way, and yelped and whimpered with pleasure at it, day after day after day, then it was indulgence run riot. I begged them to explore other groves in that vast pleasure garden to which I had given them the key.

With some reluctance they agreed. Yet they were still gripped by this idea of being degraded or demeaned during the quenching of their lust. Tying up and rough rogering was, they allowed, a somewhat crude form of it. Now they sought refinements. And again, I must admit, I was willingly seduced into ways that were as strange to me as to them. There *is* something exquisitely erotic in wearing coarse coachman's gloves while caressing the gentle curves of a voluptuous young woman; the contrast between the ancient, cracked leather and her soft and flawless skin is a sensual intoxication that has to be experienced to be believed. Especially the first time. I can still hear the gasp that Eve gave out as those gaunt ham-fists encased her hips and buttocks and pulled her to me. It forms a sweet harmony with the guttural moan from Wilhelmina when the gorgeous softness of her breasts was extruded between those weather-cured fingers by the pressure she, not I, applied.

Then Fleur confessed a long-held desire to be rogered by a man in full military dress, medals and all. Again, you see, there was that element of master and slave, which they seemed to be exploring from every possible angle. For Fleur it was the lordly, imperious male in all his plumage having his way with her fluttering, defenceless, naked body – except that it proved so confoundedly uncomfortable for her that the only possible position was with me on my back and she crawling, squirming, wriggling delightedly all over me. There was no question then as to which of us was was truly in charge.

What followed, with kilt and hunting pink, with judge's wig and gown, with policeman's brass-buttoned tunic, I forbear to record. Suffice it to say that while I bore the trappings of authority, I danced to their tune.

And that, I believe, was where their real pleasure lay. We were indulging in a curious inversion of a relationship that was already inverted. I was being "masterly" and "domineering" entirely at their whim. I, who desired nothing more than to explore to the utmost limits, the pleasures to be had by two free and equal partners, was cajoled and suborned into a position of utter hypocrisy. And yet (I must admit it once again), my own curiosity combined with the piquancy of the situation to carry me along; I was more than three-fourths willing.

Then one of them – Abigail, I believe – discovered on old Trotter's shelves an extremely rare edition of a book that I had heard of but had always assumed was like the lost books of Homer, a mere figment of men's desire. It was *Sweet Fanny's Diary*, which describes the adventures of a voluptuous and passionate young lady in Paris and Algiers back in the 1860s.

[*There follows a fairly detailed description of the contents of this classic of Victorian erotica. However, since the book is once again available to the reader – and is, indeed, published in an edition uniform with this present volume – I have cut Hornington's none-too-accurate summary of its contents. What seemed to fascinate his young pupils most was Young Fanny's description of her life in the Emir Nero's harem in 1850–51 in Sidi-el-Barrès, Algeria, not Algiers in the 1860s, as Hornington says. – FR*]

They especially [*he concludes*] liked the passage where the harem women prepare themselves in their night attire, which is designed for the Emir's easy enjoyment of all their charms, and then lie in the moonlit dark on their paliasses and wait for him to move naked among them and make his choice. Young Fanny describes it from her point of view – lying stretched out on the harem floor, her body racked by every kind of voluptuous thought and feeling; and then she explains how the Emir Nero (who was a slim, handsome, virile young blackamoor) came silently to them, stepping over their beds with his great liquorice stick proud before him, gleaming in the moonlight . . .

I agree, it is a splendidly erotic moment. Taken as what it is – a mere titillation, or a kind of libidinous sauce to season the game of love – it would do no harm. But I could see what roused *them*, my six sweet protégées. For there it was again – that master-slave connection. And here, too, was that same ambiguity, for as one reads on beyond that scene where Man is master and the women his mere chattels, it transpires that Nero is, in fact, the slave of his almost unquenchable lust for his harem beauties - not to mention the slave girls themselves, in their quarters below. The endless provocation of their availability, their powerlessness to refuse him whatever he may demand, binds him to them more securely than chains of Toledo steel. He is a prisoner on licence and his lifelong goal lies as deep as he can venture between their collective thighs. Oh yes - the *true* reasons for their delight in Young Fanny's tale did not escape me!

But that did not, alas, help me in escaping *them*. Nothing would please my sweet young jades but I must pick my way by moonlight over their prostrate bodies and kick one of them to action - five times in a row. To see and hear them, you would have thought it a life's ambition come true, instead of a new whim in one long season of voluptuous novelties. How hesitantly they rose from their paliasses - with what tremblant blend of joy and fear! How their bosoms rose and fell with the mingled passions of desire and terror. With what exquisite care did they take up the lubricant salve to anoint their treasuries of love! How tenderly they caressed their nipples until, like the girls in Fanny's story, they grew swollen with erotic longings! You see - even in such minutiae they *must* conform!

And what followed then in our own version of the Room of Joys, among a hundred silken cushions and a couple of "curiously shaped and upholstered footstools," (except that feet were the last things to be laid upon them!) was an amatory exploration of truly oriental complexity and duration. Night after night my five young pupils returned to their beds, drugged and dazed with sexual discovery - leaving me at last for dead.

With hindsight I can only marvel at my blindness. As I record it all now I see the tendency so clearly. How could I not have realized that we were even then in the grip of an aphrodisiac flood tide that bore us onward to one inevitable destination? Of course, I knew we were at the mercy of *some* kind of outer force but it seemed at the time more like an endless succession of stray currents and eddies, entirely lacking direction. Even their essays and short stories failed to alert me.

From time to time - mainly to allow my unflagging Lad the chance to recover from his pain - I recalled the fiction that we were an Academy of Love, where sweet and naïve young ladies might undergo a step-by-step initiation into the more delicate arts of venery, ha ha! I would then set them to writing little essays or short stories, in which they might indulge those fancies to which our unfolding curriculum had, as yet, offered no scope. I suppose that at the back of my mind I had some vague hope of finding that one or two of them longed to sit at her tapestry and be courted with nothing more honeyed than words. It would only take two of them to want it; thereafter, Hornington's Law of Female Conformity would have done the rest.

Here is where the warning bells should have rung:

Abigail's Story

He was clever. He could not have chosen a better moment. My master and mistress had gone to the races, taking three of the servants with them, leaving only me, cook, and the scullery maid. It was no great journey, since the course was but twenty minutes down the road. Then, about an hour before luncheon, cook found they had left behind one of the game pies and a magnum of champagne. I think she did it a-purpose, to give herself and Betty the chance to stay and see the main race of the day, which was at two-thirty. The pair of them set off just after the noon gun from the fort, leaving me alone in the house to answer double-knocks.

I had just poured myself a nice glass of port (to replace the one I had already swallowed) when there was a double-double-double knock of some ferocity. Hallo, I thought, here's some importunate wretch!

But what did I find when I threw the door open? Only the most handsome young fellow that ever you saw! A friend of my master's son from college, he says. You can have your Greek gods. He was so beautiful I almost cried just to look at him. His lips were as chiselled as the finest Lord Elgin ever brought out of Greece. His nostrils were as neat and sensitive as the best stallion's that ever left Araby's shore. But his eyes were what held me, pale, deep-set, and full of sad mystery. One glance from him and I just melted down inside. The only thing as still let me stand upright was memory.

Well, I told him where my master was and, such was my girlish folly, let slip that all the servants but me had gone there, too. At that he changes his spots! A quick look up and down the street and then he puts out a hand and pushes me roughly back inside, stepping indoors himself and slamming the door behind him. I want to tell him not to bother. He needn't be so rough. He can do anything he wants and I'll not find the power to resist him. But even then I somehow know he doesn't want me to be easy. It's take or nothing, and if I don't resist, he'll vamoose again.

So I start to whimper and beg him not to, even though my poor starved little cranny is already weeping for the feel of him. "I'm a good girl, sir," I say, just like they do in all the stories. "I've never been touched before."

He looks at the glass of port in my hand and smiles. No need for words, really, was there? But he darts into the dining room and swipes a bunch of grapes off the chiffonier. Back he comes, only to find me racing up the stairs, intend on locking myself in the first room I reach, which is my mistress's bedroom. But with those lithe, powerful limbs of his, he takes three steps to my one and his hand goes to the doorknob and closes on mine.

Oh, the touch of him! I nearly pass out, I swear. "You know this is our destiny," he murmurs, taking the glass from me and holding it to my lips.

I drink. He drinks. Then he hurls it into space. A moment later I hear it dash to smithereens on the marble floor below.

His buttons yield and out pops the most magnificent organ a girl might imagine – and of course, until now, that's all I have been able to do: imagine. But there it rears before me in all its rampant glory, the imperious master of my girlish will.

"Lead me," he says simply.

Gently, with great hesitation, my fingers close round it. The fiery heat of it almost burns! The ardent pressure of his inflamed blood seems to keep it at the very point of explosion. I open the door in a daze and, like a child with a toy dog on a leash, draw him behind me by that throbbing tree of life.

At the bed there is no ceremony. "Please? No?" I beg him as I turn. "Consider my pure, unspotted state and let me be."

But he is already pushing me back and throwing up my skirts and spreading my slim and feeble thighs with those powerful thews of his. And then, when the hard red knob of him beats at my portals, he pauses and smiles. "Shall I?" he asks. And "No!" I beg again – though my heart would break if he heeded me now.

He lowers the bunch of grapes to my lips and repeats his question.

But I can speak no more. Something in those grapes seems to promise oblivion. He tantalizes me with them as his arbor vitae down there is taunting my frail maidenhead. My lips part, my tongue reaches out, I have the bottommost grape between my teeth. I pluck it from the bunch and at that moment he pierces me.

Eighteen years of untutored longing explode in my belly as he puts his tongue in my mouth and filches my grape from me. But the next one he eats he lets me take from him. And thus we devour the entire bunch while our bodies consume each other, too, and sail away on an infinite sea of erotic pleasure.

It was too much for him. He drowned, I fear.

In dreams I mourn him still.

The End

Abigail Parkin, aged 17

And here's where klaxons as loud as Portland Bill should have sounded in one's . . . well, one can't call it a brain:

On the New Woman – by Miss G– H–

Much has been written of late on our political liberation from the tyrannous yoke of men. To those women involved in the war of the sexes, who live from one battle to the next and hardly dare raise their heads above the parapet, it must seem that the fighting will never be over. But we who do not give a fig for the outcome (surely a majority among women today) can take the loftier view. When we compare our condition now with that of our grandmothers, we must conclude that the war is already won. All over bar the voting.

But The Vote is an insignificant skirmish whose

winning will barely stir the surface of that deep pool which is the real life of woman. My purpose here is to argue that we are only now beginning to count the myriad ways in which victory will spell our ruin.

Consider how it was for our fair sex when the war of liberation was but a distant rumble, far over the horizon. Each woman could then be fitted neatly into one of two categories – the respectable and the rest. Respectable women were gentle, loving, angelic, meek, submissive, and above all, maternal. Like dear little songbirds they trilled and warbled their days away, blissful in the domestic round, admiring and supporting their husbands, comforting their children, being firm with the servants and prudent with the money – in short, making and managing the home. The title deeds to the property defined their entire universe. From New Year's Day to New Year's Eve not a single, solitary sexual thought ever troubled their breast – whose sole function was as a dairy for their latest child. For this astonishing picture we are indebted to no less an authority than Sir William Acton, the late century's leading student on all things sexual. "A gentleman," he assures us, "may draw comfort from the fact that a decent woman will pass her whole life in happy freedom from those base imperatives which our generative organs visit so fiercely upon us less fortunate men."

Well! When we consider what a vile, unfeeling crew most men are, and when we remember that our grandmother generally got only one shot at making a choice among them (unless she were very rich – in which case she got none at all), it must follow that most women ended up with a very bad bargain indeed. And from that, in turn, it must follow that most of them would have been very glad to foster this absurd fiction among their gullible menfolk, so that they might be forced to endure their clammy embraces as rarely as was necessary for the renewal of the species.

True, the men, too, had their own selfish reasons for allowing themselves to be gulled. A wife broken down with endless whelping is no match for a pretty young girl in the prime of her sexual awakening. Fortunately, the industrial-factory system, which could break women even faster then the baby-factory system, ensured a ready supply of young females in that desirable condition. The men could enjoy them, pay them, and congratulate themselves on performing two virtuous acts in one. First they had kept their wives unsullied by the base imperatives of their cruel generative organs; and second they had played their own small part in that colossal nightly redistribution of wealth which preserved the nation from the worst excesses of revolution, socialism, and anarchy.

It was not a happy system, of course, yet I venture to think it is the happiest of which we poor humans are capable. Certainly it was the happiest for all decent women. They had to endure their crapulous husbands' attentions but rarely; and they were, moreover, utterly protected from the cold blasts of economic life. And, such is the gullible, follow-the-crowd nature of women, most of our sex did, indeed, pass from cradle to grave, "in happy ignorance of etc. etc." All in all, not a bad way to live and die; many an empress of former ages has fared worse than our dear grandmamas.

But now, dear sisters, with the winning of our liberation, all that will cease. We, of his lordship's Academy of Love, know that, far from passing our lives in happy ignorance, our capacity for sexual pleasure is quite literally boundless. We do not all achieve it after the same fashion. And I – there is no point denying it – have not yet discovered the manner of achieving it at all. Yet on this we may all surely agree: that the need for sexual satisfaction is the profoundest and most compelling of all the needs we have yet experienced, young and tender though our years may be.

What are we, then? Freaks? Is this towering libido of ours some perverted visitation that has singled us out but left all the remainder of our sisters in Actonite bliss? I cannot think so. On the contrary, I believe we are a glimpse, a foretaste, of the "decent woman" of tomorrow. Poor creature! Hardly a day of her life will pass, from cradle to grave, without her experiencing the fiercest and most compelling urges from her "generative organs". But where are the men to gratify it, eh? We cannot *all* marry Lord Hornington!

If the family is to survive and the race to renew itself, we shall still - at best - get only one shot at a partner. And we shall still have to pick him from the same vile and unfeeling crew who shuffle toward us at subscription balls and spill tea and seed cake over our frocks At Home. I would liken our position to that of children born and reared in goal. Our condition became so natural to us that no other way of life seemed possible - until one day the braver of our sisters scaled the wall of our cell, peered out through the window, and informed us there was a whole new world out there.

So we fought and rebelled and were at last allowed out - only to discover that the "whole new world" was but the prison yard. But, you say, we shall break out of that in time, too. I fear so. But all we shall discover beyond is the village where our gaolers live. And beyond that? Nothing but a tiny barren island set in an infinite sea where no ships go sailing by.

What is this goal?

Its name is monogamy. Now monogamy in a woman is the most natural state in the world for a man to contemplate. For him, of course, polygyny – the tireless possession of as many vaginas as possible – is the thing. But the New Woman will not have that! I have racked my brains far into the night, searching for some way to make these expectations more reciprocal. And I have read diligently, too, among the books and papers in this house. I thought I had found it in an interesting account of some remote Himalayan tribes where each woman has four husbands and spends her days passing happily from one to the other; but it will not do for us, I fear. We poor slave-girls of Europe cannot expect to leap to such perfection of freedom all at once.

Then, on reading further, I came upon it at last – there at the very birth of our own civilization in Ancient Greece. I refer to the institution of the *hetaera* or sacred prostitute. Somehow, in all those hours and hours of my schooling that were devoted to Ancient Greece, none of my tutors ever mentioned this noble and time-honoured custom. It seems that in those days all young girls on becoming nubile were required to dedicate their bodies to the gods for a season (a few months, I believe). During that time any male worshiper could enjoy their favours on payment of a fee – which went to the god, not the girl. Their servitude was simple; they sat wearing brief, white tunics on the grass in the sacred olive grove and the men indicated their choice by tossing coins into their laps.

How wise they were, those Ancients! I don't suppose we today could revive all the mumbo-jumbo that went with the arrangement – and it would be useless petitioning the present Archbishop of Canterbury, adaptable though the rituals of his church have always proved to be. But I see nothing to prevent us from reviving the *secular* features of the institution, thereby catching up on all the fun the men have been having for as long as History runs.

I blame myself. I should have booted her out after that first day. It stands to reason that any woman as fond of pain as G– must be a thinker of some kind; I was just too stupid to realize it.

The silence that followed her reading of this essay was intrigued rather than thoughtful. Eve was the first to speak. "A few months, you say?"

G– nodded. "I suppose if a girl wanted to stay on, the priests – or whoever we get to take their place – wouldn't actually object."

"Couldn't we pick the men instead of them picking us?" Jonquil asked. "After all, men will go for anything warm and moist and with hair round it."

Everyone turned to her in astonishment.

"That's what it says in one of Horny's books," she protested.

Lord, how we roared.

Except me. I just sat there aghast, listening to them egging each other on into accepting the notion of becoming prostitutes. Eventually, in something close to panic, I slipped away and took a cab to Covent Garden. All the way I had Miss G–'s specious little essay ringing in my ears. The only unequivocally true statement in the whole thing was that they could not all hope to marry men as richly endowed as me – and that was only put in to butter me up while she slipped the rest of it past my guard.

It wasn't even well argued – not the way a man would argue it. I couldn't put my finger on any actual flaw, but that was just the cleverness of the thing, you see. The entire thing just didn't hold together. If G–

thought the gay life was a life of gaiety, she was a thousand times more ignorant than those grandmothers on whom she poured such scorn.

Thus I disposed of her arguments – somewhere near the southern gate into Regent's Park. But my gloom did not lighten. The more I thought about it, the more I saw it as a grisly kind of culmination to the events of these past weeks. Things had been going from bad to worse. I knew it, even while it was happening, yet I had been unable to put my finger on it. There was nothing I could point to and say, "There! Cure that, and the rot will be stopped." But now that Miss G– had brought us to the very pit of rottenness, it all began to fall into place.

The rot was their fascination with the idea of *compulsion* in sex. First came the desire to be spanked, then to be tied down and poked, then to be handled roughly, to be ordered about brusquely . . . and so it had progressed. What it all boiled down to was the desire to have no choice.

Choice! Yes, that was it! That's where G– was so fiendishly clever. There is a new mood of freedom among women today and though they may claim to welcome it without reserve, part of them fears the new responsibilities, the unexpected choices it will force upon them. That's what all this "Tell me what to do, darling, and I'll gladly do it," is about. They don't *want* choice! And it explains, too, their sudden fascination with the life of a prostitute – who, after all, speaks those words to everyman.

Oh, G–! Viper, vixen, and venom in my side! You knew into what hotbed of fertility you sowed your baleful seeds. Pray to the Great God Pan I will be in time to frustrate you!

It was now several months since I had trawled the

lanes and courts of the Garden for Drury Lane Vestals. As we rattled up Long Acre, I felt the ancient, happy stirring of my loins. It occurred to me that if I could pick a sweet, rosy young nymph of the pavé, I might relish her all the way back to St John's Wood. True, I ought to spend that time enlisting her to my purpose; but the prospect of enjoying a simple horn-jig once again, where all that happened would be that my boyo got a bit of snug around him, enjoyed the ins and outs of life for ten minutes or so, and gave her gravy for her giblets . . . it was too much for my shattered soul to reject. I sprang from the cab at the first glimpse of a coloured skirt.

But something had happened to those houris in the months I had been away. I wandered among them in a daze, seeing nothing that was familiar. And that was all the odder, for I knew them by name, almost every one.

Here was Polly Vaughan with the wondrous breasts, to whom I had given not six months since a revelation (her own words) of amatory pleasure such as she had never hoped to experience. And what does she say now? She looks me in the eye, bright and cheery as ever, and says, "Hello, Charley – want a nice time?"

Beside her stands Meg Brooks, not yet nineteen, whose doodle-alley has known so many visitors they have quite worn the grass away. Many take up her invitation (and her skirts) to sate their curiosity with the unimpeded view of her girlish mysteries. This same Meg swore to me I had, in my two hours between her slender thighs, taught her more in the reciprocating use of her posteriors than she would have thought possible. And what says she now? "Well then Jack, are you feeling up to it?"

Not two doors farther stands Tillie Sanders, who

told me she had turned down half a dozen offers from lively young blades to keep her for themselves because variety was the very spice of her life. And that she was never so near to paradise as in those moments before her heavenly portals felt the randy heat off a rampant new eye-opener as it drew near. But that if she had first met me, so great and varied was my repertoire of carnal sport, she might have been of a more faithful persuasion. And what does she now? I catch her in mid-yawn, which she stifles with the smile of a naughty schoolgirl and says, "Come and teach me some new games, dearie, and you won't be sorry."

When last I saw them it was winter, when kindly gaslight struggled feebly through the circumambient fogs of London's night, revealing to the lust-hounded male only what his desires desired to see. In that pitiable state I took them to my *chambre privée* or went with them to their rooms, where amorous candles or gentle firelight gilded their feminine charms. But now, in the piteous light of the dying sun, I saw a different tribe. No – that is too simple an explanation. This revelation was no trick of candle-light versus the light of day. The illumination that now shone on these drabs was the Light of Understanding. I was not here, trawling these familiar streets, looking at each Vestal through the blind eye of my smouldering Polyphemus; I had somehow borrowed the acidic vision of that odious Miss G–, my tormented young virgin. And I knew what short work she would soon make of these jades, no matter how well I coached and paid them.

I turned and sought a cab to take me from those cheerless streets.

Only then was I struck by the full enormity of what had just happened. *Cheerless* streets? But were these not my happiest hunting grounds only six months previous? How many times had I stalked these enticing courts and alleys, where the very air is charged and vibrant with sexual promise, passing by young women whose half-exposed bodies left me weak and trembling with desire – always in the hope that, just around the corner, I should come upon some fresh young peach still in the first flush of her newly excited senses?

No more! My Eden had been wrested from me. At its gate stood an angel with a fiery sword, and her name was G–.

I saw a cab just pulling up from Maiden Lane. As I hastened toward it a woman came bustling out of a doorway ahead of me and waggled her parasol to attract the driver's attention – at which she succeeded.

"Damnation!" I said, rather louder that I ought, but I was in a fragile humour by then.

She turned and I recognized, much to my surprise, none other than Miss Suzie Andrews, the faithless mistress who had run out on me from our love nest in St John's Wood. "Damnation, indeed," she said with a faint smile. "You're the very last person I wished to see."

"I can well understand that," I snapped. "Are you going to take that cab or not? Where are you going to, anyway? Who are you running from this time?"

Her smile grew a fraction broader, though it remained rather sad. She shrugged. "I don't know. Myself, I suppose. I just wanted to get away from here. Why do you smile?"

I laughed, a little against my will. "The identical urge had overtaken me."

She was always quick, my little Suzie. I grant her that. She glanced around us, at the sea of available skirt, and, turning back to me with quite a different smile on her lips – intrigued and challenging – said, "Really?"

We both took the cab; she left the choice of destination to me. "Drive us round Regent's Park," I told the fellow.

He stared at me as if I were a colonial. "Commercial vehicles not allowed into royal parks, Guv," he reminded me. I have taken so few cabs in my life – outside the charmed circle of my club, my chambers, Piccadilly, and Covent Garden, that I had never heard of the rule.

"Take us round the outside, then," I told him.

But then Suzie would not mount up, because that would take us within a quarter of a mile of our villa in St John's Wood; I practically had to go on my knees and swear to her we would draw no nearer than that quarter-mile.

Yet I think it was not my promise that persuaded her so much as some inarticulate need for my company at that particular moment. No sooner were we in the cab than she slipped her arm through mine and said, "Oh Horny, I wish you were a woman, you know. I feel we could be such friends, you and I."

The hair bristled on the back of my neck. I told her it was a most extraordinary thing but – just as with my need to escape the Garden, which turned out to be her need, too – so the identical thought had flashed through my mind. And I mean the *identical* thought. I had not wished she were a man, so that we could be such good friends; indeed, I do not believe men can ever know that closeness which can so readily spring up between two women. I had wished I were a woman, so that I could unburden myself to her.

The moment my explanation was out, of course, the necessity for so drastic a metamorphosis vanished. Then, as our laughter died, I found I was able to tell her all that troubled me – and she to listen without the benefit of that nagging parrot who sits on every woman's shoulder, screeching in her ear when she converses to a man: "They only want one thing, you know." We were nearing St John's Wood Corner by the time I had finished.

"Oh dear me, Horny," she said when I had done. "Troubles, you've gottem! But I'll tell you one thing – I think you're dead wrong to go blaming that poor Miss G–. All she's gone and done is put it into words for them. But the thought was already there, take my bible on it. If anyone's to blame – and I'm not saying as they are – it's you, my lad."

I asked her how she could possibly maintain such an assertion.

She was silent awhile and then said, "Did I ever tell you how I began?"

"I believe you did. Playing with the gardener's boy at your school for young ladies."

"Oh, that one!" She laughed with somewhat brittle merriment. Then, growing serious again, asked if I still rented the villa. When I said I did, but that there were no servants there at the moment, she said it was no matter and asked me to take her there.

"But you were so insistent that . . ." I began.

"Never mind that now," she snapped. "I've a ghost to lay – that's all." And she would explain nothing until we were arrived.

The driver, insolent lout, grinned as he dropped us by the gate. "Well done, sir!" he murmured to me as he took the fare (and tip – he made sure of that first). "I wish I had half your skill with them."

Suzie seemed relieved to find all the furniture under dustsheets and the whole place, as it were, locked away in some different time. "May we go upstairs?" she asked.

"It's no different from down here."

"That won't matter." She led the way, swinging

her hips in that unconsciously provocative manner that few woman can avoid; for once it did not provoke me.

"Why did you bolt" I asked as we arrived at the stairhead.

"That's part of what I want to tell you."

She led me to the window of what had been her boudoir. "D'you remember?" she asked.

I glanced toward the bed.

"No!" she cried scornfully, and, pointing to the floorboards between our feet, said, "Here! Standing in this window bay. Don't you recall?"

But I had given her hard for soft in every room on that floor, and in every portion of every room, and in every position, too. How should I remember one among so many?

"It was the same night," she prompted. "By morning, I'd gone."

I felt the first stirrings of some uncomfortable memory, and then an instantaneous movement of rejection within me, as if I did not wish to recall it.

"That's when I told you about the gardener's boy. Surely you can't have forgotten?"

My memory was stirring itself out of some slough of forgetfulness – but oh, with what reluctance!

"We were talking about our first-ever sexual experiences," she went on. "And you told me . . .?"

She spoke like a kindly schoolteacher, urging a pupil to do better.

". . . about my dear little Becky," I said. It was all coming back to me now.

She closed her eyes and nodded. "But you didn't tell *me,*" she said.

"I did. I remember it quite clearly now. I . . ."

"Not me," she insisted. "You stood here." She moved until she was standing right against the window, with one hand on the division between the sashes. "And you spoke to the garden out there. You spoke haltingly and low. Your breath clouded the pane. You were a thousand miles away. Not once did you turn and look at me."

I frowned. "And you mean to say you felt insulted by it?"

She made the noises and gestures of exasperation. "No! I was glad you didn't. For if you had, you'd have seen at a glance how I, too, recalled the heat of that sun-scorched grass and the woodland glade and old Mangolees and the pauper girl . . ."

I almost dropped where I stood. My knees buckled. My vision swam. There was a great roaring of blood in my ears. "Becky?" I whispered.

I don't think she had expected the revelation to have so powerful an effect upon me. The petulant schoolmarmishness deserted her as she slipped her arms about me and, giving me a sisterly sort of hug, said, "Yes!"

And I just stood there, letting the news soak in. I felt rather stupid, not being able to say a word; I merely repeated to myself, time and again, *This is my own dear Becky!* And when I did at last speak, it was to ask the most trivial question of all that waited to be answered: "But why did you feel you had to run away?"

At least she laughed. "D'you think there's the odd bottle of bubbly left in the cellar?" she asked.

Five minutes later we had thrown the covers off two arm chairs and were sitting facing each other like a pair of old cronies, a magnum and two glasses on the what-not between us. "Cheerioh," she said, lifting her glass.

"Happy days!" I replied.

She grinned. "They were, weren't they! Sun or rain, they were happy days."

"You never recognized me?" I asked.

"No more than you did me."

"Nor my name? Didn't Hornington mean anything?"

She shook her head. "You were just the master's son. I couldn't name half the masters I ever knew – no more than you could name a quarter of the servants."

I grinned. "I could name all the girls."

She nodded. "That's what I said."

After a brief silence I asked, "Was I the first?"

She laughed at the absurdity of my question. I was, of course mixing fact and fantasy, which had become inextricably jumbled in my mind. But perhaps they had in hers, too? Perhaps she had also enjoyed restrospective dreams in which we had not simply laughed and run away on that fateful day? At all events, she now spoke as if we had, indeed, consummated our maturer desires while we were still mere children.

"I remember," she said, "just lying there thinking, *He knows! No one's ever told him but the little bugger knows exactly what to do!*"

I played along with what was, after all, *my* fantasy, too. "Did that surprise you"?

"I don't think surprise came into it. Would you like to know *why* I seduced you? Because I wanted to see how young a boy could be before he *didn't* know what to do – if you take my meaning. I was always mad about boys. I couldn't leave them alone. I didn't really get any pleasure out of it – well, not much, or not often. I mean, I knew there could be pleasure in it. Watching Old Mangolees taught me that! And I did feel it myself from time to time, but that wasn't really why I did it. Why I did it was to feel the power it gave me over them. I admit that's only a pleasure of a different kind, but it's one you're more in control of, see?" She grinned at me. "You were the lucky one, Horny. I just gave it you. But the others! My, didn't they just have to pay!"

"Money?" I asked.

"Naaah! That was much later. But back in them days I'd make them wait, make them beg, set them forfeits . . . I'd promise, and then go back on my word. The funny thing was, I'd be longing for one of them to lose his temper, rip my clothes off, and force me to it. That's what I really wanted. But it never happened, not as long as they thought they'd get it willingly. Men are much nicer than women, you know. I mean most of them really do want to please us. Even old buffers who can't go all the way no more, they still like to pay their guinea and hear you moan and sigh at the touch of their finger. I can't imagine a woman crossing the road to hear a man cry out when he shoots his load." That smile again. "We're a hard lot, eh?"

I shook my head in bewilderment. It always happens that whenever I feel I am at last drawing close to an important new understanding of this most baffling obsession of mine, something like this crops up and the whole house of cards collapses.

She went on. "I think that's what your young ladies are just beginning to discover, my lord – the *power* of that . . . emptiness, that nothingness, that *hole* between their legs. But it was you put them on the way to making it, not Miss G–. She's not to blame. How can I explain it to a man?" She sighed and her eyes raked the ceiling. "I know!" Her countenance brightened. "You remember that air gun you got given – that same summer, wasn't it? Yes. Remember how you went round shooting at everything in sight? Old bottles, cats, bats in the church tower, rabbits down the warren . . ."

"The last leaf of autumn," I broke in. "I shot the last leaf out of the top of the beech tree in . . ."

"And next year?" she interrupted. "Did you do it all again next year?"

"No. Your father built a miniature rifle range down in the kitchen garden, and I used to draw proper targets, and it all got much more serious and dedicated."

"You wanted to know *how* good you was, see. You wanted to find the limits of your power."

I nodded. "And you think it's the same sort of thing with Eve and Wilhelmina and Jonquil and the rest?"

She nodded and then, gazing deeply into her glass of bubbly, murmured, "Poor little buggers!"

"Why d'you say that?"

"Well . . . the things I could tell them."

I let a long silence elapse before I said, "Why not?"

I gave my word of honour as a gentleman that I would spend the evening at the club; it was the only condition upon which Suzie (as I still thought of her) would agree to meet my young students and pass on any part of her wealth of experience. I decided to walk it, at least the length of Lisson Grove; it was so long since I had taken any exercise – of a vertical kind. My tread was lighter than it had been for weeks; I had not realized what a hermetic little world my six young mistresses and I had created between us, nor with what unstoppable momentum they had usurped my manly right to guide and command their sexual progress. Ahead of me lay an evening among my fellow men, entirely devoid of the company, the concerns, the foibles, the *demands* of females. Time, in short, to pause, step back, and take stock.

However, I had not reached the corner of Lords

cricket ground before fresh doubts assailed me. What *was* Suzie going to tell them? With something of a hollow gut I realized that the only sexual exemplar they had in common was *me*. What was she going to say about *me?* It struck me then that, as their teacher - no, more than that, as their guide and friend, their protector in a world that would revile them for the choice they had made, I owed them a particular duty that transcended my more general obligations as a gentleman who had given his word.

Indeed, as a gentleman, I had no right to give that word. *That* had been the despicable act. To keep it now would only compound the treachery. I turned about, crept in by the tradesman's entrance, and asked good old Nimrod to find some place where I might conceal myself in comfort (suspecting that he had availed himself of a hundred such opportunities since our removal to this house). I was not disappointed, but it was to the Colonel that I owed my success. His heyday in this house had been well before my time. Indeed, while he was playing high-cockalorum here, I was probably lying on my tummy beside young Becky, watching Mangolees and his doxies rogering away.

Anyway, it seems that the Colonel had taken thought for the morrow - that sad morrow which comes sooner or later to all who devote themselves to the delights of Venus: the failure of our potency, transient at first, permanent at last. Against that day he had mined the house through and through with a variety of secret passages and spectating chambers. There he could lie at his ease on silken divans, drink his port, smoke his havanas, and watch younger and fresher blades at play through mirrors of ingenious silvering.

I was caught out by such mirrors on my first visit to a high-number house in Paris, when I was eighteen.

One of the most voluptuous young ladies of that very costly establishment whispered in my ear that she had taken an instant and overwhelming liking to me – which I was naïve enough to believe. When her heart was stirred in that way, she said, it was her custom to grant the stirrer the freedom of her person with no obligation to pay. Indeed, she would feel highly insulted if I offered her anything beyond the beauty of my body, et cetera, et cetera. Of course, I never for one moment suspected that my companions had paid and were all the while enjoying a ringside seat. Still, I had the last laugh for she could not go back on her pretence without giving the whole show away; only when I raked her giblets for the sixth time and she fainted in voluptuary delight did she earn her release. That little exploit gained me such a reputation as a libertine that even had I lived celibate since, I should still be pointed out in whispers.

I was therefore surprised that the multiplicity of wall-mounted mirrors in the Colonel's house, together with the discrepancy between its outward dimensions and the internal measurements of the individual chambers, had never excited my curiosity. I could only surmise that *that* particular faculty in me was already too excited in other directions. But I comforted myself with the reflection (pardon me) that if the suspicion had not occurred to me, it would hardly cross the minds of my sweet young charges. Of Suzie I was less certain. To a whore, a wall-mounted mirror is always an object of deep suspicion. But perhaps she had satisfied herself before my arrival, for never once did she look my way except to pat her locks and prink out the folds of her dress. Certainly if she suspected I was there, she could hardly have said some of the things she did.

They were dining in a most leisurely and informal

manner, serving themselves and each other to avoid being overheard by the servants. I could not help smiling to see how solicitously Miss G– canvassed the opinion of her onetime maid, Miss Abigail Parkin, as to whether she preferred these grapes or those, and then cut and washed them for her with exquisite care. Libertinism is the greatest leveller, which is why tyrants hate and fear it so.

It was, however, my last amusement for the evening.

"What d'you think of our lord and master?" G– (of course) asked when they were well fed and feeling convivial. "Is he not one of the greatest lovers of women who ever lived? And are we not the most fortunate of females to have come under his mentorial wing?"

"That's a new name for it!" Suzie replied with a laugh. Her sharp little eyes quickly scanned the others, gauging their response.

They laughed, a little nervously. But they laughed.

Emboldened, she continued with a sigh: "Yes, my dears, I fear he is a very good lover, as men go. You are, indeed, hardly likely to find better – and you may take it from one who has tried a thousand or more."

After that, what could they do but defer to her; it was a flankonade to get in so early with her vast experience.

"Why do you speak like that?" Eve asked.

"D'you not know the man?" Suzie asked pugnaciously.

"Very well, I think."

"Then he's not the man I know, if you can take that tone. Do you know that rampant prick of his, which he can will to stand and stand and stand again? Even when tears of agony stream down his face, he can still force himself to outdo the smartest guardsman and stand to attention and drill for hours more."

"Yes?" Eve responded, as if she were still waiting for the objection.

Suzie stared at her in bewilderment. "Well, how does that make *you* feel? When you have given your best and lie there, weak and fluttering from the pleasure you have taken of him, and up pops that gristly ruffian between your thighs and goes nosing into the your softest parts once more?"

At this I had expected my dear young scholars to pipe up and say I had done them pretty well in that line, thank you very much. They had measured out their gratitude to me in a hundred thousand sighs of pleasure these weeks and months gone by; surely now they could repay the debt? Even at a quarter per centum it would drown out the perfidious siren Suzie.

"I have to allow," Wilhelmina said, *as if* reluctantly, "that he has often left me somewhat . . . played out. It is as if he has taken even more pleasure than he has given." She spoke as if that were a heinous crime in any man.

It was all Suzie had been waiting for. "You put your finger on the wart at once, my dear. Great and untiring lover though he may be in a purely physical sense - and I would be the last to deny him that - he nonetheless fails lamentably in all other respects. Men are fond of assuring each other that women exist solely for their pleasure - just as we women are apt to go about telling our uglier sisters that they are 'looking utterly charming today.' Is it not so?"

A titter of laughter rippled among them.

"The truth," she continued, "is precisely the opposite. Our ugly sisters go on being ugly, and men drag out their luckless existence, whose sole purpose is to pleasure us women. Men know it, really. In their heart of hearts it's the only thing of which they're sure.

That's what I was trying to get old Horny to see in the cab on our way here. I was telling him about old dodderers in their dotage who can't raise it half an inch. But still they come to us. Still they hand over their five guineas . . . ten guineas . . . whatever it is . . ."

"Ten guineas?" Abigail gasped.

Suzie looked her up and down. "You'd get that easy, my duck." She said it almost as an aside.

A horrible suspicion began to grip me in the guts.

"Why did you leave him in such haste?" Miss G– asked earnestly.

Suzie, who would eye a hundred guineas with suspicion, did not know what to make of her. She knew the girl was too bright to be so artless, yet she could see no sting in the tail of this question.

"Yes, why?" Eve repeated, miffed, no doubt that Miss G– should make use of information that had come from *her*.

Suzie looked at each in rapid turn. "Tell me," she said at length, "have you never had one of those curls that will not stay in place?" Her pause forced a murmur of assent. "You do your best with water, pomade, macassar oil . . . you even despair and send out for axle grease." A ripple of laughter. "And nothing serves. Back it comes for more. And doesn't it drive you to despair!"

"You mean Horny's like that?" Miss G– asked disingenuously. (At least, *I* could see it was disingenuous.)

"With only one woman to please him," she replied heavily, looking round to be sure they got the point. "Perhaps, with six of you . . ."

"Five," Eve said with a sweet smile at Miss G– – who simply smiled back and told her not to be so modest.

Suzie, afraid the argument was slipping from her,

went on, "I don't know if any one of you has any designs on the man, for herself, I mean, when her days at this academy are done? But be warned by me."

"I don't follow," Jonquil said with genuine uncertainty. "What is so terrible about a man whose capacity is even greater than ours? Surely it's more pleasing to find the soldier still willing to stand and drill, as you put it, than to have him limp and useless?"

There were nods and murmurs of assent.

Suzie smiled pityingly. "I thought so, too, my dears. My first week with him – now I still account that the happiest in my life. There was nothing my imagination and experience might suggest but he was ready to outdo it in feeling and ingenuity. My last night in his bed – the night I decided I had to get away or die – I believe the pleasure of his loving almost tore me limb from limb. I never knew such a rendering of my senses before or since. Certainly not since. But no matter what I did, there he was again – that damned disobedient lock of hair, springing back for more. Well, I tell you, a girl's dignity can only take so many insults of that kind."

"It's true," Jonquil murmured. "I've often thought it, too – without, you know, *actually* being aware of the thought. It's been sort of lurking there in the background, waiting to be thought."

Eve nodded, eager to counter Miss G–'s implied slur. "Last night, just when I was thinking surely no mortal man could desire more of a girl than I had just given our dear master, he turned me over and started to take me again from yet another angle."

I almost burst through the glass in my fury, for, of course, it had been Eve herself who, having almost fainted with her pleasure and pausing only to recover her breath, turned her back to me and wriggled her slim little bottom in against my protesting creamstick with orders no honourable soldier could disobey – and then had the gall to fall asleep sighing her ravishment . . . and with no thought of pity for me, who had two more private tutorials to give before I could sink into the same happy slumber.

"But how are you better off now?" Miss G– asked evenly. "I mean, how many men do you have in a day? And is not the last of them as . . . I mean, is it not as if a different curl kept springing up and clamouring for attention? And is that not worse than endlessly favouring the same recalcitrant lock?"

Suzie pursed her lips and smiled all round, recruiting their agreement in advance. "Let's forget this talk of locks and curls, my darlings. You all know what I really mean. You've all given your best to dear old Horny, many and many a time, I'm sure. And you've seen him leave you, randy as ever to get his end up some other one of you. Now maybe you never realized it could be different. Why should you – especially if he's the first man you ever let inside you in all your lives? So maybe you never felt that . . . what can I call it? Disappointment? No, it's worse than that. It's a sense of failure. It's like something inside you, telling you you've failed – as a woman. Be honest now – haven't you *never* felt that? Not even once?"

Being women, and eager to get these trivial little questions out of the way so they could hear something of real importance – which Suzie's eyes promised every time they alighted on one or other of them – of course they murmured their heartfelt assent.

"I knew it!" Suzie cried triumphantly. "That's because you're real women, see! It's there in each one of us. It's like we're born with some inner knowledge of the way things ought to be, between a man and a woman, when they've had their fill of melting moments. The man should be exhausted and useless. He's shot his bolt and lost his pride. He's a tamed and docile little babby. That's the way it should be."

"And the woman should be ready for more?" Miss G– began in scorn.

Suzie held up a finger. "Yes and no. Nothing's ever simple about us women, is it! She should be ready for more and at the same time proud he hasn't got it to give her. Proud she's beaten him to a frazzle." She turned to Miss G–. "You asked how many men I have in a day, being in the trade I am. I'll be honest with you now. Mondays it could be two – or none. That has happened on a cold, wet night in winter. Saturdays it could be eight. It could be more but eight's enough. Taking one week with another, you could say between two-and-a-half and three dozen . . ."

"That's over a thousand men a year," Miss G– said in alarm.

"At ten guineas each?" Abigail asked with bated breath.

Suzie let her tongue linger on her lip – without actually answering the question, I noticed. "The next question is, do I take my pleasure of them all? And the answer is no, of course not. Nor even half of them. Nor even a quarter. Once a day, more like it – but that's enough for any woman when she knows there's plenty more where it came from."

"And the others?" Jonquil wrinkled up her nose.

Suzie pointed a finger at her and smiled, as if she had just asked the most pertinent and intelligent question of the evening. "I wouldn't say it's no pleasure with them, but it's pleasure of a different kind. It's the pleasure of seeing the mighty brought low, of taming the beast – and of knowing you did it all just by the power of your own sex, and without so much as a flutter of feeling. *That's* where Horny – dear man that he is, and I won't hear a word against him - but that's where he's doing you all a great wrong. He's destroying your pride as women - pride in the absolute power of your sex to get the last laugh on any man. On all comers, as we say!"

She glanced around, wondering if this were the moment to deliver the *coup de grâce* - and decided it was. "Just imagine it, my dears - something you've never seen. A randy young stranger standing before you with his piledriver in your hand, hot as a furnace and rearing to go. And ten minutes later . . . twenty . . . whatever you bargained for . . ."

"As short as that?" Wilhelmina burst in with surprise.

Suzie nodded. "Ten minutes later it couldn't lift the skin off a cup of cold tea. And you could hide it all behind your little finger. But *you!* Why, bless my soul, you're already tripping downstairs to take on the next, and the next . . . and leave them all like dishcloths. That's the pleasure I'm talking about. The pleasure of power. Men call that warm haven between our thighs the hairy oracle, the dumb glutton, and a million names beside. Well, I tell you - she has the wisdom of a dozen oracles and the appetite of a hundred gluttons, but . . ."

She did not need to finish the sentence; even I could see the notion taking shape among them: *As long as we are Hornington's mistresses, we'll never know that ultimate joy.*

"What can we do?" Fleur asked with a sort of hopeless sigh.

Suzie smiled at her, almost pityingly. "You are women," she reminded them. "You'll find a way - now that you know what prize awaits to crown your success." She looked around at the decor, as if for the first time. "D'you know, this would make a superb brothel, this house. A very, very high-class establishment, you understand – patronized exclusively by the aristocracy and their guests.'' She cleared her throat. ''And d'you mean to tell me that six such fragrant young flowers as you could not bend his lordship to your purpose?''

Never had I been so glad to see so many trousered legs, or to sink into so much padded leather, or to catch the whiff of so much manly sweat.

''Hallo Horny,'' cried Tosser Morgan. ''How was Africa?''

''Dark,'' I reassured him. No use trying to drive bees out of Tosser's bonnet.

Later, Stoney Miller asked me if I was really cured at last. I told him, no, I was still in the thick of it, worse than ever. No idea what he was talking about, but there's no point in being pedantic, not among friends.

At last, the man I was waiting for came in – a curious, rather intense chappie called Adcock. Took no end of a ribbing on account of his name, but took it in good part. He flopped down next to me and asked if I knew the score.

''Hundred and twenty-eight for seven,'' I told him with, I hope, a suitable air of gloom. I don't follow cricket too closely myself but I'd seen it chalked up by a newspaper boy on my way in.

''When did they draw stumps?''

''Six,'' I guessed. Certainly there had been no sounds of snoring as I had passed Lords at six-fifteen. ''Funny you should ask me the score, Adders, old bean,'' I went on. ''I was just about to do the same to you – on a point of law, don't you know. You're some sort of legal johnnie, aren't you?''

''Something in that line,'' he admitted. ''Professional enough to charge for it, anyway." He eyed me warily.

"Quite. I was wondering about Mohammedans, you see. They can have four wives, can't they?"

He grinned and relaxed, thinking this was going to be a joke rather than a solemn professional consultation. "Believe they can, old boy. Not a bad wheeze. Plus houris and all that."

"And when they come here – as ambassadors, men of business, and so forth – that johnnie in a turban who bought all those guns off Vickers last year, for instance – do they, er, bring all their wives with them?"

He shrugged and shook his head.

"Put it another way," I persisted. "Would there be any legal bar to their doing so?"

He shrugged again. "As long as they don't do it in the street and frighten the horses, I don't suppose there is."

"Ah!" I sat up and began to take interest. "So what you're saying is that your average Abdul bin Abdul, as long as he keeps his nose clean and doesn't go flaunting it about – he can import all the bint he wants and the law won't touch him?"

Chaps all round were beginning to prick an ear by now.

Adcock grinned even more broadly. "What's all this about, Horny? I never knew you to take such a lively interest in international law before. Damme if you haven't got *both* eyes open for once."

"Oh . . . nothing," I replied airily.

But the swine wouldn't let me go. "Come on! There's a purpose in all this. Thinking of turning Mohammedan yourself, are you?"

"Who told you?" I asked fiercely.

"By jove!" cried Kinloch-Shand. "Hole in one!

You've hit the nail on the head, Adders. Is the club's most confirmed bachelor about to be pressed for bigamy, we ask ourselves?''

That set up quite a cry, of course. The mathematical geniuses among them pointed out that a full-blood Mohammedan could get away with trigamy, or even tetragamy . . . or whatever you'd call it. Double bigamy, Adcock called it.

Those howling cads, they simply dragged it out of me, and before I knew where I was, I found myself spilling the beans. Not raw, of course, but well cooked. I reminded Tommy Champion of our bet, which made him look pretty sick – and then went on to confess that the laugh was on me.

''Before I went into hiding,'' I said, ''I had these four absolutely stunning young ladies, all of whom had burned their boats behind them – no hope of going back and resuming a straightforward middle-class life, you see – just hanging round my neck, simply begging me to carry out the original proposal. Fleshpots of Europe and all that.''

''You said Africa,'' Tosser Morgan accused me.

''Slip of the tongue,'' I assured him. ''Turned right instead of left at Calais. Anyway . . .''

''So you've really been hooting around Europe?'' Stoney Miller accused.

''No!'' I roared. ''If you'll just shut up, I'll tell you. My man Nimrod reminded me of that house I won of dear old Trotter, if you remember.''

''In Aberdeen,'' Champion said.

''Well, that's what I thought. Apparently it was – *is*, I mean – in Aberdeen Gardens, Maida Vale.''

Eyes lit up all round at the mention of the name.

''So I took them there. But I did a bloody foolish thing. I promised them that I'd teach them every amorous trick in the entire lexicon of lechery. And when I'd finished, I said, the aristocracy would come battering at their doors, begging to marry them."

Hoots of disbelieving laughter. Cries of, "You put your foot in it there, old boy!" Et cetera.

"And now they want to hold you to your word?" Adcock guessed.

"No!" I cried, aghast. "I want to keep my word by marrying all four of them myself! *Now* d'you understand?"

Stunned silence. New doors opening on very rusty hinges, revealing new depths of understanding . . . suggestions of God-knows-what delights.

"I tell you chaps," I shook my head sadly and spoke to the carpet between my feet. "You have never experienced the like of those girls. Think now - just try to remember - the most skilled and luscious and lascivious young nymph who ever parted her thighs beneath you. Or upon you, or beside you, or in every way imaginable and unimaginable alike. Think of *her*. And now think of the sweetest, most angelic, most demure, most virginal young beauty who ever brought tears of frustration to your eyes. And now imagine them *as one and the same person!"* I sighed and shook my head at the ineffable sadness of things. "It's no good. There are simply not the words in the language to describe the combination."

"And they're all four willing to marry *you?"* Champion asked in angry disbelief.

I gave a crafty smile. "Not going to tell them," I said. "Thought I'd pop into town, get myself converted to Mohammedan somewhere, slip back out, and do all that stuff with the henna and boiled sheep's eyes and fifty cups of coffee. I think that's the wedding ceremony. Something like that, anyway. Get it over and done with before they twig what's happening. Tell them it's some new sexual novelty." I smiled gloatingly. "I promise you fellows, I never met four young ladies more eager and willing to try out litle novelties in that line. *And yet they remain perfect ladies all the while.*"

I could see a fair bit of slavering going on, so I thought it was time to wind up the proceedings. "For isntance, you'll never believe what little romance we've dreamed up for tomorrow night. I don't know if I can pull it off, mind, but I'm going to have a jolly good try." If I'd kept it up much longer, I'd have been deafened by the sound of eyeballs popping out and bouncing all over the floor. "They want to pretend they're young ladies – all of blue blood, mark you – who've been abducted and forced to work in a brothel. The good old white-slave fantasy. I don't know if any of you were ever inside old Trotter's House? Number thirty-four Aberdeen Gardens? Quite an ordinary place on the outside. But inside it's like a Parisian big-number house. I never saw anything so opulent. So, in terms of setting, it's going to be a bit of a downhill canter. The question is, can I pretend to be six different customers to all six young ladies?"

"Six?" Everyone shouted at once.

It woke Adcock from some private reverie; he began clapping and calling out, "Well played, sir!" before he twigged it wasn't that sort of six.

"Yes, two of them brought their ladies' maids with them. And I tell you – if the mistresses are like fresh-churned butter, the maids are like double-boosted cream." I looked across at Adders. "You don't know of a religion that lets you have *six* wives, I suppose?"

When I returned to my little harem, now augmented by Suzie, who had elected to stay for a while, they were so sweet and obliging (except Miss G–, to be sure) that I knew at once some mischief was afoot.

Until now, I had never enjoyed more than two of them at a time. I don't know why. Squeamishness, perhaps? There's something *natural* about two girls to one fellow, whereas three-to-one seems like the sort of trick a nouveau-riche would get up to – the sort of cad who'd keep ten footmen up all night to welcome him home with the dawn (and couldn't name one of them). But now, prompted, I'm quite sure, by Suzie, they had taken it in their mind to forgo their own ultimate pleasures and give me "the night of a lifetime", as they put it. All five of them and Suzie.

I have been in big-number houses in Paris with two dozen absolute stunners near-naked about me; I mean to say, the *déshabille* of a *fille d'amour* on her own territory leaves nothing to the imagination. But I had never before stood at the centre of even half a dozen fully naked young creatures, all of whom were in that deliciously defenceless condition for my delectation alone.

They crowded close but without touching me. But they were touching each other like billy-oh, turning slowly and beginning to sigh with an almost ritualistic intensity. I ran my fingers gently over them at random as I and they spun and wove; I touched every curve and swelling that was offered in that bewildering and heady parade of female loveliness. Old One-eye was up like an otter at dawn, unable to believe his luck, beating like a hot club against my navel.

It was Abigail who began it. Over the past weeks she had developed a trick of procuring what I can only call a miniature orgasm. Often I will merely touch her – and this will be at the very beginning of a long and pleasant orgy together – I do no more than touch her, or caress her hair, and I will see her eyelids fall as her eyes flicker briefly upward, and a barely perceptible spasm of shivering will run over her, from her neck to the soles of her feet. And she'll smile sweetly and murmur, "There! I just came." And so she continues throughout our session together, enjoying, perhaps, a hundred of these petty thrills before the Big One engulfs her and leaves her gasping and exhausted.

She began to do it now – that little upward lilt of her eyes and the almost imperceptible spasm of her flesh. I had never mentioned it to any of the others. Indeed, it was my sternest principle never to say anything that might be construed as the slightest criticism; and with young girls like that even the most factual statement, such as "she has red hair, yours is dark," can be turned into a damning indictment. But there is a sort of sexual telepathy that sparkles between women when they are excited, so that, whether they actually saw it or not, they soon became aware of what was happening to my darling little Abigail every time my fingers lingered on her flesh.

It is more than telepathy, in fact. It must be a sort of tele-kinesis, if there is such a word; and if there isn't let me invent it now to describe the way in which one girl's emotions can *move* another's as they jointly approach the extremes of their passion. Soon they were all at it, shivering with petite orgasms and eyeing me with a kind of desperate surprise, as if they wondered where such thrills had been hiding all those months during which we had seemed to explore every last aspect of sexual delight.

In Suzie's eyes I detected true despair; the souls who are damned into hell in medieval paintings show just such dejection as hers. She stared at me in glum mortification, much as to say, "I had forgot. I had forgot." She is one of those women of powerful passions, quite unable to govern her unruly libido once it gets control of her – and yet so ashamed of it after that she will go to almost any lengths to contain it against a future explosion. I believe her going on the streets was, in a strange way, her most successful ruse in that direction. For no girl of ordinary sensibility can respond in the slightest degree to the vast majority of the men they are forced to entertain. And in Suzie's case, that very lack of response must have seemed the chief reward of each encounter, reinforcing as it did her self-declaration that she had "overcome it at last."

But now, among my five trembling beauties, she was learning how paper-thin was that shell of indifference. What she had forgotten was that benign and delightful hysteria that stirs young females when they are excited and aroused, and to which even the dryest and coldest of them cannot help but respond. Suzie was now lost in the power of its grasp.

As that strange, collective intoxication overcame them, they nudged and pressed me toward the bed – the largest in the house, of course – and required me to lie down flat on my back. There one of them gently squatted over my face, tantalizing me with the occasional touch and firmer caress of those most darling folds of all. One kneeled on all fours at my left, another at my right; and while they caressed my chest and suckled at my nipples, my hands were able to explore their free-swinging breasts, their soft bellies, and the moist, excited clefts between their legs. A fourth engulfed old Polyphemus with her mouth or nether treasure – and in my condition I could not tell which. The others caressed me where they could.

If it sounds unfeeling to identify them merely as "one" and "another", I must add that they swapped places so swiftly and in so random a fashion, that the only one I could be sure of at any given moment was the one whose privities I could see and taste – for by now I knew their dear little mossyfaces as well as the ones they showed to the world.

I thought I had experienced every variety of sexual pleasure until that night; now that I look back on it, I wonder I had not tried it before. We men are so accustomed to thinking of that joy as centered on our cocks. We see that column of gristle as a proud beacon, radiating joy over the rest of the landscape that is our less sentient flesh. So, at least, I had thought of it until then. Women, I believe, have no such precise locus for their delight. True, their excitable flesh is very much in the same, or corresponding, place as ours; but the thrill itself, when it comes flooding over them and pours through their sinews does quite literally that. It both enters and emanates from every corpuscle of their being. They feel its palpitations as violently in their throat and chest as in the backs of their knees and the soles of their feet.

That night, I believe I came as close to experiencing an orgasm of that female type as ever man may venture. I came in the fingers that were lost in ecstasy in those two dumb gluttons. I came in the arms that were pinned beneath their gorgeous bodies, which squirmed over me incessantly, like excited little puppies. I came in the nipples that suffered such sweet torment in their babywarm mouths. I came in the face that strained upward for living burial in that fragrant bower of all our joys. I came in the belly and thighs to which such unseen and unimaginable stimulations were applied. In the throes of that violent orgasm, which both racked and flowed from my every part, the great spermspouting orgy of the usual organ passed almost unnoticed. I came from the topmost tingle of my scalp to the utmost curling of my toes.

Now, with the calm clarity of hindsight, remembering that ultimate and unrepeatable experience, I cry damnation on all those women who might avail themselves of such delight, both day and night, and yet do not - though to each of them there are a thousand willing men to give them the chance. Damn them, I say, who so treacherously neglect the paradise they carry around within their bellies. Damn them who by their neglect permit its delicacies to grow rank and bitter. Damn them that they die never having known what it is to live. And damn those of my own sex, too, who have assured "decent" women that such a paradise is neither nice nor theirs to possess - for women are so eager to conform they will believe it at once.

On that night, however, these higher philosophical reaches were beyond me. And in that respect I was more like an octogenarian man than any female I have ever known. For women, once roused, are ready for a whole one-night season of engagements; but men will flag after the first triumph. And that night, for the first time in my life, I joined the regiments of my own sex. My grand ladies' lollipop lay limp on my sweat-washed belly; even my lank hairs had more power to rise than he.

Suzie could not believe it. She whooped and crowed like a hyena, saying, "We've done it at last!" and "What did I tell you, girls?"

Oddest of all, I didn't care a toss. I just lay there, replete and exhausted, staring up at my six sweet nymphs, feeling more benign and more at peace with the world than ever before in my life. My gaze ran up and down their glorious young bodies - a sight that would, at any other time, have me rampant again in seconds - and I felt nothing for them but a great warm glow, a sexless love that would have embraced them in neuter joy until we fell into oblivion.

And then Dr Johnson (for so I call him when he'll

bow to none) spoiled the idyll. I suppose he has a pride of his own, which pays no heed to his master's finer feelings. Whatever the explanation, there he was, hoisting himself up with arthritic weariness, throbbing away, getting all hot and bothered once more – and damn the pain it gave me.

"No! Oh no!" Suzie left off crowing.

"And what did I tell you?" Wilhelmina almost had a fit with her laughing.

Eve rose like some great sea creature, all ponderous and blubbery, and, lifting a thigh and stretching wide her labia, engulfed the Lad with her soothing warmth. Her attitude was one of noble sacrifice on behalf of her sisters; but soon a more ancient response began to awaken within her – or, rather, to rekindle, for she had already tasted more than one night's share of the ultimate intoxication. Her jaw fell wide; strawberry blotches glistened in the sweat that bathed her breasts and abdomen; she began to fight for breath.

The others took fire from her and soon we were back at the old disorder of our flesh. I was heedless of the pain and exhaustion while that imperative thrill of my most tender flesh held sway. And it was the same with them, too. The conspiracy that had ruled them earlier – to give me the supreme and unrepeatable climax of my life – was forgotten now; it was every girl for herself. Or, rather, every honeypot for itself, for I believe they were now as ruled by their genitals as I was by mine.

There were two of them behind Eve, drenching my thighs with their love juices and working themselves into a fine lather there. Two others squatted hard over my clenched fists, impaled on my thumbs, and made a quivering joy of every move and angle I could devise. And as for my face, well, I fought for air against the marauding of a Cupid's furrow that seemed possessed of but one desire: to give me the most easeful suffocation a man may imagine.

Six wild young bacchantes – and I in touch with each only at her holey of holies. The friction of flesh and juice – the sap of their ecstasy – was like the crackle off a distant rifle range; and the sighing of their throats as they rose from one peak of pleasure to the next was like an undiscovered music that might one day furnish a requiem for an emperor.

It must, I suppose, have ended in another orgasm for me; but again it was like none other I had known before. My limbs and extremities – including that most delightful extremity of all – seemed to be stretched into a kind of infinity, which was a new plane for all such joys. And my seed appeared to flow out of me like a vast, slow river at its confluence upon the sea, with nothing to hinder the union.

And so they all collapsed upon me, and one another, and sighed, and clasped their limbs about me, and wriggled gently and sluggishly, and shivered again in that delightful way of theirs while they wound themselves down from the peaks of their *plaisir* through the lesser thrills of what Fleur once called *petits souvenirs d'extase*.

I believe we may all have fallen into a spontaneous slumber. My next memory is that the windows were dark and the candles two inches lower. They were all wide awake and chattering like monkeys. It seemed to be an argument about whether they had "managed it at last."

"Go on!" they encouraged Fleur, who was sitting cross-legged with her shins against my left thigh, leaning slightly forward over me. They were all staring at the Lad.

He was now a mere two inches of shrivelled skin, like the pelt of some small, burrowing animal with the flesh removed. The foreskin through which he was usually so proud to burst and show the world his scarlet fever of desire was like a crumpled dunce-cap and every bit as pale.

"D'you think it's safe?" Fleur asked warily.

"He's awake," Abigail cautioned.

"Now we'll find out," Suzie said ominously. She smiled at me. "It was safe while you slept, anyway."

"What's all this nonsense about *safe?"* I asked.

Jonquil laughed. "We're determined to get the better of Old One-eye here."

"Or die in the attempt," Abigail added with a show of weariness.

"Well," I groaned, "You've won. Any death that may have occurred is on this side of the battlefield."

"Are you sure?" Suzie asked suspiciously.

"Word of honour."

It was an absurdly dangerous thing to do in full hearing of the Lad, of course - to talk of *honour*. I realize that now, but at the time he seemed so dead to the world I could not imagine he'd overhear. Yet the moment Fleur took her courage - and the Lad himself - in both hands and began to squeeze and tickle him experimentally, I knew what a ghastly mistake it had been.

"No!" I cried in despair.

"It's all right!" Fleur encouraged me - for, of course, the first little spasms of rekindling delight that I could so clearly feel had not yet translated themselves into that rush of hot blood which turns the Lad into such a fine, upstanding fellow.

"Stop!" I warned her. "If you pity me and value your own beauty sleep, stop this minute!"

But it was too late. The Lad was already up and about - not exactly a ramrod yet, but a passable swan's neck.

"Damn, damn, and damn again!" Suzie cried. "Just when we were so sure!"

"D'you think . . . if we left it?" Fleur suggested timidly.

Suzie shook her head. "But we'd always know. We'd never be able to look ourselves in the mirror and say, *we did it!"* She sighed and slipped off her dressing gown again. "Back to work, me deeriohs!"

If there's one creature in all the world with whom I can now claim to feel some direct and visceral sympathy, it is Dick Turpin's horse, Black Bess. When she dropped dead, having carried him at a nonstop canter from London to York, I now know *precisely* how she felt. I never thought I should gaze at six such gorgeous young female bodies, all eagerly disporting themselves with me in the most lascivious possible way, and feel nothing but an exhausted loathing for the entire female tribe. I never thought I would pray for a physical impotence to match that which now seized my spirit.

I did nothing. I simply lay there - sapped, debilitated, spent, burned out - while they frigged themselves delirious upon me yet again. And yet again I was made excruciatingly aware of the absolutely sexual superiority of women over men. For though they had earlier thrilled themselves to a standstill, and would have sworn that not another tremor lay within them, their excitement and arousal now worked its self-hypnotic magic and they rose again in mutual hysteria to another explosion of orgasmic flesh, with a chorus of cries and ejaculations, tears and laughter, as if they were fresh from a week of abstinence.

But this time I did not join them. My prayers for impotence were granted at last. And there, with Eve stretched out upon me, working her buttocks like a man and, with each firm thrust, hissing in my ear,

"Shrivel, damn you! For pity's sake shrivel!" – the miracle happened. Never before had the Lad gone to sleep on the job. But there he was now, slack and shrivelling, falling softly from Eve's dear little moey.

"I did it!" she shrieked in triumph – which she hastily amended to, "We did it!" as she rolled off me and the other craned round to gape in wonder.

And there he was, wet and gleaming, and all curled up like the bud of a fern in spring. There was a silence you could have bottled and sold to a library. Fleur gulped heavily and whispered, "*Now* is it safe?"

"Now it's safe," I moaned in reply.

They kissed him, licked him, sucked him scarlet. It might as well have been my big toe for all the joy I felt. What else they tried I do not know for, in the middle of it all, I fell into a slumber so profound I did not waken for almost twenty-four hours.

And what awakened me was the hearty sound of male laughter – and laughter of that special kind which declares it to be both provoked and shared by females of a like mind. Almost before I was fully awake I realized what had happened: My little ruse with the fellows at the club had succeeded only too well. It would have been perfect if I had been awake to receive them and prod their dear, dim-witted minds in the intended direction.

I rose on one elbow, drawing in a breath to groan at the pain I expected to feel. But to my astonishment I felt none. I looked down at the Lad and eased him tentatively away from his scrotum. Over these past few months – taking my new trade a professor of venery as seriously as I do – I have favoured him with all the attention a stable lad would give a thoroughbred during the flat season. By now I know all his moods and ways – things about him no ordinary fellow ever bothers (or needs) to learn.

For instance, I know that if he had a sleekly gorged appearance, even when slack, then he's ready to stand and serve on a prodigious scale; in such a state I may conduct private tutorials with each of my pretty young pupils, one after another, and with no complaint from the Lad. But if he's limp and pale, if I can feel my opposing fingertips through his gristle when I grasp him lightly, if his head is slightly too large for his neck . . . then he's off his oats and I'd be best advised to draw the line at two or three of them only. Worst of all is a state to which I have never, in fact, allowed the chap to descend – a limp, lifeless column topped off by a painfully bruised and swollen head. I have, however, read of it in a book I once picked up in Wych Street – and I fully expected to find that the previous night's excesses had at last brought the Lad so low. (Though a swollen head would certainly have been justified, I might add!)

Well, I'll say one thing for a good long sleep – some of the things it knits up are a great deal more important that the ravelled sleeve of care. I swear I never saw my dear old chum looking so sleek and gorged. *Come now,* I thought to myself, *you're in fine fettle for some competitive sport among the other Lads from the club.* And I swung my legs out of the bed.

It was then that I heard the key turn in the lock.

I smiled happily – for, of course, I could leave the room by way of the secret passages at any time. Indeed, it might suit me very well for them to suppose I was safety locked away in here when I was, in fact, free to watch and study them all at my whim.

I was humming a merry little tune and feeling about in the gloom for my slippers when I became aware that I was not alone. I had assumed that whoever locked the door had done so from the outside. Now I heard the rustle of silk sheets behind me and I knew that my gaoler was my bed-companion, too.

"This room reeks like a brothel," Miss G– murmured.

A sequence of absurd responses rose to my throat:

"You!"

"Now see here, Miss . . ."

"Kindly explain . . ."

I uttered none of them. Instead, I found myself overwhelmed by a strangely concentrated lassitude. It was the like feeling that people call *déjà-vu* except that this was more like *déjà-compris*. That is to say, I had no feeling of having done and said these things before but, as each event unfolded, I was gripped by the most powerful conviction that something within me had already performed that accommodation to novelty which we call understanding. What happened between me and that strangely dearest of all my sweet young nymphs thus assumed an air of inevitability; once it had happened, I could not imagine the slightest variation, much less an alternative.

I slipped back between the sheets and stretched out at her side, not touching her at any point. "Let me out?" I wheedled. "I promise I'll come back. But I must make sure of one or two things out there."

"There's no need," she whispered. The musky perfume of her skin was more aphrodisiac to me than ever.

"But you don't understand."

"I understand everything."

Now I did indeed groan, not with physical weariness but something much worse – that doomladen prescience of defeat which attends all my *verbal* intercourse with women. "I'd like to believe it."

"Well," she began, "I know you're just about the cleverest and sharp-wittedest man I've ever met. And, most unusually for such a creature, especially one born into the purple, you're also just about the kindest, too. The only thing I don't know is whether you planned it all out from the beginning or whether inspiration comes to you as you go along. I hope it's the latter. In fact, I'm sure it is. Your shrewdness is all very spur-of-the-moment. You're not at all calculating."

I put my lips to her ear, whispered "Blather!" and withdrew.

"You mean," she continued, unruffled, "that my essay on the delights of sex-slavery didn't send you scurrying off to Covent Garden? And you *didn't* pick out poor Suzie – who, as you must know, is your bounden sex-slave until the end of time, and who loathes every particle of her yielding body for being so – you *didn't* deliberately select her to come here and try to steal us away from you? And you *didn't* know she'd try to do it by turning your young ladies into whores? And you *didn't* seize upon it as your means of introducing the husbands you intended for us all along?"

I just lay there and stared at the ceiling. When she put it like that, I had to admit, at least to myself, that I had been deuced clever about the whole thing. However, I was also rather glad that she was there to point it out, as it hadn't actually struck me until then.

"Rather tell me," she concluded, "that your name is not Hornington – for *that* I'd sooner believe." Then, sweet as the silk between which we lay, came the *coup de grâce:* "And who – as a matter of interest – did you intend for me?"

"That's been my greatest puzzle all along," I admitted ruefully. "You know how it is when you find an odd earring in the bed? And you run your mind back over all the girls who might have lost it there? Coral? Daisy? Evelyn? Annette? Stella? And for one wild moment each of them seems possible – until a bit of cold reason slips in and says otherwise? Well, that's how I've tried matching *you* with every bachelor I know with the slightest drop of blue blood in his veins. There just is no one.''

''Well, well, well,'' she said – and even in the dark I could *hear* the smile on her lips. ''That must mean something.''

She didn't need to say any more; she just lay there, radiating that musk, and waiting for my hair to stop standing on end – which it did, sooner or later. And the force that had kept each lock erect all drained out and concentrated in the one most obvious place.

And by that uncanny instinct of hers, Miss G– felt it happen. We were a foot apart and lying motionless, yet she felt the Lad grow hot and hard, reaching silently towards her, beating to the sudden gallop of my heart. ''Yes!'' she whispered, stretching all four limbs as wide as they'd go. ''It's time at last.''

I did not wait, in case the same humiliations awaited me as before. This time I did not miss Cupid's One True Highway.

It was like no other passage of love I have ever experienced. When I was a solitary lad I used sometimes to long for my *Doppelganger*, as the Germans call it, to come sneaking into bed with me (whenever I slept unaccompanied, that is). No one else would know half so well how to trip those secret springs of my ultimate pleasure; no one else would accept half so readily each new and surprising intimacy that I might offer.

It sounds the damndest thing to say, I know, but the night I spent with Miss G– was not simply close to that experience – it *was* that experience. My childish wish for my double had matured into . . . well, I have to admit it, into the first truly adult sexual experience of my life. How can I describe the difference?

With every other girl there has been, as it were, *two* pleasures in the one act – hers and mine. They may have overlapped, but never completely; there always remained some irreducible fraction of each that would not merge with the other. But it was not so with Miss G–. Perhaps my experience of the night before, which I likened to an almost-female orgasm, had prepared the way – for I certainly experienced it again with Miss G–; and yet it was not (as it had been before) *my* orgasm, but *ours*. The pleasures of the journey and the ecstasy of arrival were ours; the very notion of trying to separate them would have been absurd.

The other difference is that once was enough. My former desperation to come and come, to indulge the Lad to what one might call the "Black Bess limit", was gone. With Miss G– I seemed to have slipped into a different time scale, where opportunity could not be measured in minutes and hours but rather in years. We lay a long while in each other's arms, saying all the sweet nothings that did not actually need saying at all.

At last I murmured, "I'd best do the rounds, you know. After all, I am the principal of this learned establishment."

She chuckled. "D'you suppose they haven't locked the doors – just as we have done?"

I let her use of the royal pronoun pass, for it was now my turn to chuckle. "Follow *us,*" I said, as, dressing-gowned and slippered, I slid aside one of those innocent-looking mirrors and led the way into the labyrinth.

The first we saw was Abigail with Lord E–y, the Marquess of B–'s son. They were naked, but half-covered by the disordered bedclothes, and he was holding a bunch of grapes over her lips and staring into her eyes with the stupidest expression I ever saw.

Eve was fast asleep and all in a tangle with Clarence Kn–x-R – by – not, strictly speaking, a member of the aristocracy, though his family has turned down more offers of a peerage than is decent; they practically own the whole of W-ckshire and pride themselves on being "England's premier untitled aristocrats". More interesting to me was the *way* they lay together – *so* tangled in each other's limbs. No man sleeps thus with his whore.

Wilhelmina and young Lord V–rt were still at it, with her lying spoonbacked into him. To look at their heads, side by side on the pillow, you'd swear they were deep asleep. Only the slow, regular thrust of his hips and the slight, gyratory response of hers gave their game away. "They look as if they could keep at it for ever," Miss G– whispered.

Brian F–st–cs, from the *Almanac de Gotha* rather than *Debrett,* was standing at the window with Jonquil at his side. They were staring up at the moon. As we were about to pass on he turned and, raising her in his arms, carried her back to bed.

Fleur lay fast asleep, her pale and beautiful face framed in the dark, curly mass of her hair. Lying at her side, half-raised on one elbow, was David D–dale, Lord W–k's boy, transfixed by her beauty, sighing his heart across that infinite, two-foot gulf between them.

"D'you know the wisest thing of all about you?" Miss G– asked as she took me by the girdle and tweaked me back to our room.

"Just a moment," I replied. "What about Suzie?"

"I'll tell you about her in a mo," she replied calmly. "The wisest thing about you is that you know how to use sex to *enhance* one's life."

I laughed. "That's about as clever as knowing how to use water to slake one's thirst."

But she did not laugh. "Don't you believe it," she assured me. "This world is simply crawling with people whose only use for sex is to blight and destroy. But in fact you already know that, don't you? You know how it was with me before you came into my life - how I was almost destroyed by it. And yet, instead of slinging me out on my ear as any other sensible man would have done, you just waited patiently for the magic to do its work."

"Did I?" I asked as we stepped back into our chamber.

She kissed me gently on the tip of my nose. "Why do you always pretend to be the world's biggest dunce?" she asked - with, I noticed, a slight edge to her tenderness. "That's something we'll have to cure."

"Tell me about Suzie," I reminded her as we slipped back between those deliciously silken sheets.

"I think," she replied slowly, "after we're married, she'd make a good companion to me."

"After . . . what?" I asked. There was a great, empty feeling inside me, which I mistook for dread.

"Surely you know?" she asked.

"Know what?" I tried to wet my lips but my tongue was too dry.

"It is our destiny. It was written at the dawn of time. You and I, my dearest, are about to embark on an erotic adventure the like of which the world has never known. Even you, with your vast knowledge and experience, will be astounded by the discoveries we shall make together - once your ring is on my finger. Our little Academy of Love will become the merest Dame School to the University of Erotic Experience we shall one day found."

I was shocked into silence, but it was not the shock of an unaccustomed thought. Nor an awkward thought. Nor an alarming thought. It was the shock of knowing that she was right. And behind it, something more subtle – that shock of realizing I had known it for some time without being aware of it.

"Yes," I said at last.

"Yes, what?"

"Yes . . . mistress?"

"N-o-o," she said patiently, drawing out the word.

"Yes . . . my lady?"

She snuggled contentedly against me. Normally the Lad would have leaped at this fresh opportunity but he lay there snug and seemingly content with his portion. I hope *that* was not what she meant by her talk of erotic novelties.

"D'you truly mean it?" I asked her after a while. "About Suzie?"

"Every word," she replied. "She has so much to learn." She chuckled. "How odd that I, who was a virgin until a few moments ago (in body at least), can say that of her, the plaything of a thousand men! And yet it's true. And it's also true that there's only one man in the world who can set her free."

"Tell me," I interrupted, "why would you need a companion?"

"For when we go round the world, of course."

"Eh?"

"Surely you realize that an understanding as great as yours, coupled with a collector's instinct as great as yours, coupled with a capacity for sexual indulgence as great as yours . . . cannot possibly be allowed to moulder in these islands?"

"It can't?"

"Of course not! That's what I said just now. Do pay more attention. Together, my darling, we shall span the globe, savouring its amorous delights, proving its forbidden pleasures, devouring its most arcane joys. And by *we* I mean you. Me. And Suzie." She made three sentences of it, as in a story to a child. "And when we return, we shall write such an account that the whole world will go on fire at it!"

I lay back and, slipping my arms about her beautiful, slender body, pulled her to me.

"Goodnight," she murmured, closing her eyes and settling happily against my chest.

It was a very *firm* sort of murmur.

And as she fell into slumber she whispered, "My darling, darling husband."

THE END

Postscript

"Hornington" was, in fact, Lord Hennington, Earl of Rutland; the nickname, naturally enough, was conferred upon him at Eton and it stuck for the rest of his life. He was the eldest son of the Marquess of Effingham and succeeded to the title in 1919. The name was, in itself, the source of yet more ribaldry at that illustrious school. It would make an interesting study someday – the effect of names and nicknames upon their bearers. How do people called Smellie go through life? What does a man called Onions feel about eating onions? Is there a Hitler family still in Germany? More to our present purpose: Would Hornington have been the sexoholic he undoubtedly was if his name had been, say, Littlefellow, or Priestman?

"Miss G– H–," who became his wife (an intention she formed the moment they met), was Guinevere Hedgecoe of Glasgow (not Edinburgh); the thin disguises, which he applied to his other "pupils", too, are typical of his aristocratic disdain for thoroughness. I may add that it made all of them fairly easy to trace to their living descendants. He kept his promise to them. All were finally married off to aristocrats, even Suzie, after the world cruise. Indeed, she did rather well, for she married above the rank of Earl. To say more would soon identify her to anyone with access to the *Debretts* of the period. However, such are the rules of descent in the UK peerage, most of the descendants are now commoners again. For their sake I shall refrain from identifying Eve, Wilhelmina, and the other girls here. I shall only say this: Without exception their descendants are noted among their friends for their sanguine natures, their anarchic domestic arrangements, and their cheerfully liberal promiscuity. Dear Lord H, dead these many years, lives on in the power of his example.

The house in Aberdeen Gardens – indeed, the entire street – was destroyed by a V-bomb in 1944. It had fallen into neglect and was empty at the time, but between the wars it was known as "the millionaires' knocking shop". The basic price of a lay there was £50 – at a time when £400 was a goodish annual salary for many a professional man. Even so, it was a spiritual comedown from the libidinous heights of Lord Hornington's time. He sold the place to a White Russian countess after the Great War; as Madame Zezia she turned it into the most opulent and expensive brothel in England, a rival to the fabled *6 rue des Moulins* in Paris.

Potent though he was, Lord H. was almost certainly infertile. A sexologist friend suggests (not entirely seriously) that from the onset of puberty his lordship never gave his testicles enough time to build up a fertile load. "The man seems to have found the pressure of a few dozen spermatozoa quite intolerable," he says. "So he ejaculated them at the first opportunity into the nearest available woman – not one of whom ever got enough to do the trick." Well . . . perhaps.

Lord H. himself must have suspected he was infertile; he behaves as if he were quite certain of it, though that was also in the tradition of his family. His father, who was (quite obviously) not infertile, bought silver bowls wholesale at Asprey's, which he filled with guineas and gave to any local country girl who bore his child. He also pushed hollow spheres of gold into their vaginas before he bedded them – Casanova's old trick – telling them it prevented conception. They were not deceived, of course, but it ensured a ready supply of wenches for his bed.

In later life – as his physical prowess waned, one suspects – Hornington became rather solemn and "preachy" on the subject of sex. In fact, until this lost manuscript came to light, that is how most remembered him: an earnest and aging gentleman who seemed to like nothing better than to chair endless public debates on the therapeutic and cathartic virtues of sexual activity. He contributed the most monumentally unreadable chapter (on sexual taboos in Micronesia) to the utterly unreadable Swedish Symposium of 1928, *Acta Sexualopatologica*. A sad ending for one whose earliest contribution to the literature of sex was as fresh and enjoyable as this present volume.

How, then, did it come to light? There is no evidence that Hornington tried to suppress it during his lifetime – quite the contrary, in fact. His only act of censorship was to go through it and physically excise his wife Guinevere's name wherever it appeared. He used a razor blade and cut himself more than once, as blood on widely separated pages testifies. (I could not, of course, physically punch a corresponding hole in the printed page; instead, I have adopted the cipher, Miss G–.) That small degree of self-censorship is in itself evidence that he wrote the bulk of the manuscript more or less as it happened, putting Guinevere's name in full; only when those peculiar "schooldays" were over, when her marriage to him becomes a kind of *fait accompli*, did his sense of honour constrain him to go back and expunge it.

Thereafter, he seemed almost indifferent to the fate of the manuscript. One of "his" children (i.e., Guinevere's by one of her numerous lovers), a man I shall call Lionel for the good reason that that is not his real name, told me he remembered it knocking around one of the nursery cupboards for years. Originally it had been held together by bootlaces tied through punched holes. Then one day, when somebody urgently needed a bootlace and there was no other spare, it was scattered to the four corners. Alas, some of its pages have gone the way of all nursery junk. The rest might have followed it but for one of those chances that seems to have attended so many erotic manuscripts down the years. People can throw away or burn Shakespeare's manuscripts – John Evelyn describes seeing one of the Bard's descendants actually doing so – but let there be the smallest salacious hint in the matter and people will carry it with them to the far ends of the earth.

The carrier in this case was a Miss Laetitia O-. She died in the forties but she has a brother and a sister still alive. Lionel was highly amused to hear that Miss Letty had done any such thing. "My mother took it into her head once that our upbringing had grown rather lax. She was absolutely right, of course, and her remedy was beyond criticism. Miss Laetitia was *everything* her name suggests: prim, with a starched blouse and a high-button collar, pince-nez, an air of permanent disdain – even her *teeth* could frown at you. Oh yes, and she had a bike with a back-pedal brake. She left our employment when I inadvertently overheard her farting – when she thought she was alone, you know. She could never face us again after that. But I never knew she took the pater's old jottings with her. Well, well, well!"

In fact, she did more than take them; she painstakingly reassembled them into their most logical sequence – no easy task, I may say, especially as they were originally scribbled down on any scrap of paper that came to hand, from perfumers' bills to (in one case) an advertisement for a temperance laxative. There were even two dunning letters from tradesmen to Colonel Trotter, the former owner of the house. But with infinite patience Miss O– reassembled them into the order I have presented here.

But where did she do it, you ask? To answer that (and preserve the most astonishing bit of the story to last) let me leap forward to the present day and describe how the papers fell into my hands.

Since my equally astounding rescue of the two *Fanny* manuscripts (published as *Sweet Fanny* and *Sweet Fanny's Diaries* – uniform with this present volume), I have learned to beware of strangers who write to me with the exciting news that they, too, have discovered some long-lost erotic gem and would I like to help them get it published? In every case these supposed gems have turned out to be the vapid maunderings of semi-literate sexoholics born no earlier than 1960. So when Capt Bill Knox- Rideout of the Royal Signals wrote to me saying he had discovered what purported to be an erotic memoir of Lord Hennington's, I did not exactly fall on his neck with gratitude. There were, however, two hopeful features. First, Knox-Rideout is, of course, a well-known Falklands hero – the sort of man who hardly needed to court extra acclaim as the restorer of this small piece of erotic arcana to the nation. Secondly, he claimed to have discovered it *in the Falklands, during the campaign!*

One quick phonecall to Lionel, whom I had already consulted on other aspects of his father's work, established a surprising but incontestable connection with that remote corner of the South Atlantic – for Port Stanley is where Miss Laetitia O-chose to live in her retirement! As soon as I saw the manuscript, of course, any lingering doubts were dispelled. No one could have gone to such pains to assemble so many and such varied scraps of paper from around the year 1904, *and* found inks of that vintage in which to concoct the forgery, *and* have counterfeited the Etonian handwriting of the 1890s with such artistry; and even having done so, he would not then virtually *give* the thing away, saying that his true reward would be to know that thousands might enjoy it as he had done. A hero indeed!

As to the writing itself, both in form and content . . . well, it has all the charm – and the pitfalls – of a thoroughly amateur production. It's a matter of taste, I know, but for my part I would rather read a dedicated amateur of erotic writing than the most polished professional. True, the pro knows precisely what he's about. He (and it usually is a he) moves the story with consummate skill. He never lets the pace flag. He knows how to put you on the edge of your seat and he keeps you turning the page. And yet . . . and yet. Somehow, in all that human dissipation, the humanity gets dissipated, too.

Amateurs, as their names implies, are still too much in love with their subject to allow that to happen. This present manuscript is a perfect example.

Hornington obviously knew what an erotic book "ought" to be like; he had read enough of them to reject most with scorn, and rightly so. But he knew there should be a *My Earliest Awakening* and a *A Young Courtesan-to-be is Prepared for Her Deflowering* and an actual *Deflowering* and a *Flagellation* thrown in for good measure. So he gives us all of these. Fleur's tutelage in her aunts' brothel is pure invention, I feel; the rest are lavish embroideries of quite common childhood and adolescent experiences. But he has no idea how to gather them into a single coherent narrative; each is a separate gem in a completely realistic setting that jars most oddly with the stereotyped episode it is supposed to support. A pro would have related them all to one central character and tied each of these "obligatory" tropes into that character's development.

The result of Hornington's "method" is that one reads in a delicious state of tension that is in itself mildly erotic. One is never sure whether one is now embarking on some obligatory element of erotic fiction or a piece of genuine autobiography. Usually, because he's a lazy writer who would much sooner reach for a genuine experience and embroider it, rather than go to the trouble of inventing everything, like a *proper* writer, the result is a titillating mixture of the two.

Or so I trust the reader has found it to be.

One loose end remains to tie: the erotic round-the-world voyage that Guinevere promises in the closing paragraphs. It certainly took place, and Suzie – as I have already indicated – went with them. They departed for Paris in 1904 and returned via Glasgow in the winter of 1906. But if they kept a record of what must have been a momentous journey, all I can say is that it has not yet come to light.

But who knows? Perhaps these words will stir some reader to recall a sheaf of fading papers that have mouldered in the attic for as long as he or she can recall . . . In this small corner of literary arcana it is far too early to write them off.

Faye Rossignol
Crouch End

More Erotic Fiction from Headline:

Sweet Fanny

The erotic education of a Regency maid

Faye Rossignol

'From the time I was sixteen until the age of thirty-two I "spread the gentlemen's relish" as the saying goes. In short, I was a Lady of Pleasure.'

Fanny, now the Comtesse de C---, looks back on a lifetime of pleasure, of experiment in the myriad Arts of Love. In letters to her granddaughter and namesake, she recounts the erotic education of a young girl at the hands of a mysterious Comte – whose philosophy of life carries hedonism to voluptuous extremes – and his partners in every kind of sin. There is little the young Fanny does not experience – and relate in exquisite detail to the recipient of her remarkably revealing memoirs.

Coming soon from Headline
SWEET FANNY'S DIARIES

FICTION/EROTICA 0 7472 3275 X £2.99

A selection of bestsellers from Headline

FICTION

TALENT	Nigel Rees	£3.99 ☐
A BLOODY FIELD BY SHREWSBURY	Edith Pargeter	£3.99 ☐
GUESTS OF THE EMPEROR	Janice Young Brooks	£3.99 ☐
THE LAND IS BRIGHT	Elizabeth Murphy	£3.99 ☐
THE FACE OF FEAR	Dean R Koontz	£3.50 ☐

NON-FICTION

CHILD STAR	Shirley Temple Black	£4.99 ☐
BLIND IN ONE EAR	Patrick Macnee and Marie Cameron	£3.99 ☐
TWICE LUCKY	John Francome	£4.99 ☐
HEARTS AND SHOWERS	Su Pollard	£2.99 ☐

SCIENCE FICTION AND FANTASY

WITH FATE CONSPIRE The Destiny Makers 1	Mike Shupp	£3.99 ☐
A DISAGREEMENT WITH DEATH	Craig Shaw Gardner	£2.99 ☐
SWORD & SORCERESS 4	Marion Zimmer Bradley	£3.50 ☐

All Headline books are available at your local bookshop or newsagent, or can be ordered direct from the publisher. Just tick the titles you want and fill in the form below. Prices and availability subject to change without notice.

Headline Book Publishing PLC, Cash Sales Department, PO Box 11, Falmouth, Cornwall TR10 9EN, England.

Please enclose a cheque or postal order to the value of the cover price and allow the following for postage and packing:

U.K: 60p for the first book, 25p for the second book and 15p for each additional book ordered up to a maximum charge of £1.90

BFPO: 60p for the first book, 25p for the second book and 15p per copy for the next seven books, thereafter 9p per book

OVERSEAS & EIRE: £1.25 for the first book, 75p for the second book and 28p for each subsequent book.

Name ...

Address ...

..

..